Ava Episode Three

Odette C. Bell

A Galactic Coalition Academy Series
Ava
Episode Three

www.odettecbell.com

www.odettecbell.com

Free Books, Full Series, & Fulfilling Endings

Love free books?

All Odette C. Bell's series start with a free book, so you can try before you buy.

Love a complete series?

There are over 70 complete series to check out.

Crave uplifting, fulfilling endings?

Odette's books blend action, wit, and a dash of romance and philosophy to bring together character journeys you'll never forget.

With over 70 complete series from fantasy to sci-fi, why not start your next favorite read today?

www.odettecbell.com

Chapter One

LEANA'X KEPT THROWING HERSELF AGAINST THE invisible shields, but they wouldn't let her pass.

Sweat caked her brow far faster than the space suit's internal environmental controls could let it evaporate.

She kept screaming until she was hoarse, until it felt as if her throat would be torn from her neck.

But none of it mattered.

She fell down to one knee, then the other, bringing her hands up, trying to beat the shields, but they wouldn't shift. Nor did they burn her or rebuff her backward, sending her skidding over the stone floor behind. These were not ordinary shields, and this was no ordinary palace.

She had no idea how long it took until she gave up, her arms falling between her legs, her shoulders hunched down low, her head drooping down until her chin almost rested against her chest.

She began to sob, began to cry, until large salty tears streaked her cheeks.

There wasn't a goddamn thing she could do. Worse?

The connection between her and John... she couldn't feel it anymore.

That bridge seemed to be closed.

Leana'x, Prime Queen of Artaxan One, brought her hands up, buried them against the visor of her helmet, and broke down.

...

Prince Maqx

He stood there and stared at the vault door, his head held at an angle, his eyes never closing.

... He could hear them.

The Force.

Just a fragment of them in his mind. Not enough of a direct line to hear what they wanted. But their greed? Ah, that came through as clear as possible.

It twisted through the Prince's body. It reached his hands, made them curl into such tight fists, he felt his Replacement body stiffen like smart concrete.

He took a step back from the vault door, his head spinning.

For what felt like the trillionth time that hour, he brought up his wrist device and activated it. In a blink of light that looked like a mini flash of lightning flickering over the device, a hologram appeared over the machine.

It was an update. On Admiral Jones' life.

... The Admiral was still alive. But his life signs were stressed. He was fighting. What, the Prince couldn't tell.

He watched the readings with all the focus of a man waiting to see if he would live yet another day.

Though the Prince should be rooting for the Admiral to win, the Prince was not.

He was waiting for the inevitable – for the twisted, cracked Replacement mind of Admiral James Jones to break under the pressure.

And then the Prince would happily take his place at the head of this operation. It would be better, for everyone. For the Prince already had a plan.

He just needed the time and space to enact it.

He stood there for god knows how long, watching the Admiral's fight vicariously.

Though the Prince didn't know who the Admiral was fighting, it was clear he wasn't fighting the new Prime. So perhaps it was the useless Commander who'd become her sole protection in this harsh galaxy.

The Prince took another step back from the vault door, then another. He finally wrenched his gaze off the hologram and locked it on that imposing structure once more. His orders were clear – he wasn't to leave this spot. For this was a time sensitive mission. Even if they didn't know when the Prime would die and AVA would finally be forced to retreat to the Prince's body, Maqx couldn't afford to leave. For the split second AVA arrived was the split second he would have to gain entry into the vault.

For within the vault was everything the Force needed to finally break the wall that held them back from the Milky Way.

And then, finally, the full invasion would begin.

The Prince stared up at those massive shielded metal doors for several more seconds. Then he turned away.

Just one swift movement on his polished boot, and he left his position.

He strode down the empty hallways of the Prime building, the echoing pound of his footsteps the only sound in this imposing structure.

He rested his neck back, cracked his spine and shoulders, and smiled.

He had a feeling – a feeling that the Admiral's plans would backfire. And when they did, the Prince would be ready. He would get a head start right now, so that he – not the Admiral – would see this mission through to the end.

Chapter Two

Leana'x

SHE SAT THERE IN FRONT OF THE SHIELDS FOR GOD knows how long, just nestled there, her head against her knees, her eyes brimming with tears as she rocked back and forth, back and forth.

The only sound in this lonely stone palace was her bones as they creaked and the never-ending echo of her sobs.

The tears didn't just streak her face – they covered them.

To think, she could feel this much crushing emotion at the passing of a man she'd once hated...

"We don't know he's dead yet," she spat at herself, but her voice was all twisted and wrong.

She was being pulled in two opposite directions. In her heart, she wanted to believe more than anything that the Commander – despite the crippling odds against him – would have had the skills to defeat the Admiral.

But her head told her something else. All those years of

Academy training told her there was no way John could have survived against the Admiral's next-generation technology.

Leana'x rocked back harder now, finally unhooking her arms from around her legs. In a moment of pure desperation mixed with gut-punching tension, she slammed her fists into the stone ground around her.

This wasn't fair.

... But she couldn't stay here like this, sobbing her heart out as she waited for the Commander to come.

She had to get up, crawl through the palace, find something to help her.

Because she couldn't forget one thing. Even if the concept of losing John was as brutal as being eviscerated by a space bull, a far worse fate would wait if the Admiral found some way of getting in here.

She'd... she'd seen his ship. The way it had been tiny at first only to grow. Technology like that shouldn't exist in the Milky Way. She'd never seen anything like it, let alone heard about it from any of her friends in tech development.

And if it was that powerful, wasn't there a possibility that the Admiral would be able to use it to break into this apparently impenetrable palace?

That thought galvanized her, finally saw her rock up to her feet.

She was shaky, so she had to stagger to the side and lock a hand on the wall.

It, like the rest of the palace she'd seen so far, was made out of stone. Not fancy stone, mind you – ordinary rock.

As she inclined her head over her shoulder and looked behind, the tunnel looked like it was out of some old Earth ruin, not the most sophisticated palace the Artaxans had.

... And yet she couldn't deny the feeling of the place, could she?

As Leana'x forced herself to take a solid step forward, she felt a thrill of nerves race up her spine. They sank hard and fast into her jaw, making it feel as if she'd been stupid enough to chew on a live wire.

She tried to shake off the weird sensation as she took another step forward, then another.

She was injured, tired, going crazy with grief, and yet, the distraction of this place was enough to draw her forward.

She emptied out of the relatively short tunnel she was in until she reached a set of stairs. They were sweeping and led down from a mezzanine level to what looked like an atrium below.

She paused with her hands on the railing in front of her. She twisted her head from side to side as she tried to take in the whole place at once.

One thing was growing abundantly clear – this was a building unlike any she'd ever entered. She'd never felt anything close to the feelings that were now exploding through her. They were so exquisite and powerful, she felt like they'd take her over completely.

She brought her hands up and tried to lock them on her arms, rubbing them up and down as she chased away the sensation. But the sensation wouldn't shift, and her hands wouldn't grip.

She kept walking forward. Her arms were loose by her sides now, as if someone had unhooked them from her shoulders.

... It felt like something had hooked into her heart and was dragging her forward.

She went down the stairs, entered the atrium, then didn't stop.

She twisted around and headed into a room that was directly in front of her.

The door looked like it was made of nothing more than stone, but as she approached, it shifted to the side without a sound.

Inside, it revealed a room.

The first room she'd clapped eyes on that wasn't completely made of stone.

... It had equipment in it – panels, computers. She didn't recognize the design, but she could hear them softly humming and see the reflected light of a screen on the opposite side of the room.

The screen was on some kind of standby mode, but as she took a step over the threshold of the door, it turned on with a buzz. It was a specific buzz – one that didn't just power through the room, but sunk into her too as she tried to take a surprised, jerked step backward.

But that would be when her back slammed up against the door. It had reformed behind her without a sound.

She turned suddenly on her foot, throwing herself toward it. She brought up her hands and struck them against the stone, but the door wouldn't open, and her attempts to hit it did nothing.

Leana'x took a lurching step away from the door.

She was trapped.

...

Commander John Campbell

The fight was frantic.

But it didn't last.

Though John's armor gave him absolutely everything it had, though it pushed him to a place he'd never been, it just wasn't enough.

It couldn't be enough. Admiral James Jones had an entire prototype vessel with all of the weaponry that entailed, and John had nothing more than his bio suit.

John expected the Admiral to kill him – expected one well-placed ionic blast to slam right through John's back, tear through his armor, and extinguish his body as if it were nothing more than a valiantly flickering flame.

But Admiral Jones wasn't in it for the kill. Instead, he disabled John.

Using the vessel as a battering ram, he slammed it against John's back, sending John skidding into the pock-marked moon surface until John's entire form was pinned. It was like having an anvil on his body. No, it was far, far heavier. There was not a goddamn thing he could do as he was pressed relentlessly into the dirt but scream. And boy did John scream. He gave it everything he had, his lungs practically shaking, and yet, the scream wasn't one of true sorrow.

Because Leana'x was fine.

He'd retained a connection to her up until a moment ago, then it had shifted. Almost as if something had blocked off the bridge that now existed between them. Kind of like a shutter slamming into place, blocking out the view from a window.

Though John could barely move, at least he could open his lips, and he screamed her name with everything he had. It reverberated through his helmet but could travel no further.

He waited.

One second, then two, then three.

His eyes were plastered wide, his head covered in a thick sweat his armor had no hope of evaporating.

And he kept waiting.

For the inevitable. It should come any second. He knew that. There was only one thing Admiral Jones would do. No questions. No second chances.

But death did not come.

John tried to incline his head to the side.

That would be when the Admiral finally appeared.

In a haze of light from a transport beam, the likes of which John had never seen, Jones appeared right there in front of John.

John didn't beg. Not a single word. There was no way he was going to give this Replacement bastard the satisfaction of knowing he'd won.

Instead, John set his jaw as hard as he could while still cracking his lips open. "You might kill me, but there's no way you're going to beat the Coalition. They will come for you. Mark my words, they will come." John's words blasted out with all the combined fire and passion his beating heart could manage. And that was a hell of a lot considering these would likely be his last words.

... But the Admiral still didn't do it. He didn't attack. He could. As John's eyes sliced down to the Admiral's belt, he could see the gun holstered there. It was a make John didn't recognize, but one that possessed inherent power. Just with a quick scan from John's armor, he could tell that a single bullet would be enough to completely pulverize John's body.

And yet, the Admiral still didn't fire.

That would be when John finally noticed the guy's eyes. Wide. Fixed on John. The quality of them... completely goddamn terrifying.

John had seen a lot in his life. From his parents dying to the numerous skirmishes he'd fought on behalf of the Coalition – but what he saw in the Replacement's eyes shouldn't damn exist in this galaxy.

And that was the point.

For as John's eyes widened as far as they could until the skin could've cracked and opened up the muscle beneath, he realized he was catching a glimpse of the Force.

His breath stilled, his heart stopped, and he watched.

The Admiral finally reached a hand forward. With his wide-open gaze locked on John, it was clear Jones had just come to some decision.

John, it seemed, wouldn't die.

No. The Admiral had something much worse in mind for the Commander….

…

Admiral Jones

This made so much sense. More sense than killing the hapless Commander.

No. It was much better to access his mind, his body, his armor, and, more than anything, the unique connection he'd formed with AVA.

For now Admiral Jones was in front of the Commander, the Admiral could sense it. The armor the Commander was wearing wasn't normal. It had been upgraded by something. Something not familiar to the rest of the Milky Way, but something easily recognizable to the Force within the Admiral.

AVA.

She'd somehow stretched between the new Prime and

the Commander. How, the Admiral couldn't tell. But that didn't matter.

No. All that mattered was accessing that connection.

This was so much better than anything the Admiral could have hoped for.

For this meant he could access AVA directly without the meddling help of the useless Prince.

Jones had started this, and now he could end it with his own hands.

The Commander wisely chose not to fight as the Admiral leaned down, locked his hands on the Commander's collar, and dragged him to his feet by his armor.

Though the Admiral couldn't see into the Commander's eyes through the opaque visor of the Commander's armor, that didn't matter. Just holding him, the Admiral swore he could feel Campbell's fear.

So powerful. The kind of force that could shake right through a galaxy and remake it anew.

"... What are you doing? If you expect me to talk, you're dead wrong. I won't tell you a thing about her," the Commander's voice was even up until the word *her.* As soon as he referred to Leana'x, his voice sounded as if someone had shoved his throat into ice.

It was clear the Commander had feelings for the Prime.

Which was good.

For it meant when it came to killing the Prime, it would be easier. She wouldn't see it coming.

The Admiral shoved his hand forward, and as he did, he maintained his mental connection to his ship. He commanded it to begin the transfer process.

An alteration of the basic transporter technology the modern Milky Way was built on, the alteration process borrowed heavily on Replacement technology and the footprint of the Force.

There would be nothing the Commander's armor would be able to do to stop it.

The Commander seemed to pause as a red light shot out from the ship and encased him.

Then the man screamed. So deep, so shaking, so soul-crushing. It sounded like the Commander was having his brain ripped right out of his skull.

The Admiral did nothing but smile. A wide kind of smile he hadn't had cause to show for so long. For it had been weeks since things had been going this well.

For finally, finally the end was in sight. An end better than anyone could envision.

In that moment, the Admiral wasn't connected to the Force. If they ever tried to press into his mind again, they would do so much damage, the Admiral would be ripped asunder like a rock under the impact of a meteorite. But it didn't matter; the Admiral knew this was the right path. His masters would sing his praises for this.

The Commander continued to scream, his voice now so hoarse, it sounded like it would crack. And crack it did as the man was suddenly pulled right off his feet.

The Admiral took a step back and watched the Commander as the red light from his cruiser locked the man in place. It suddenly spread the Commander's arms wide, almost as if it were getting his measurements. And in many ways, it was.

Replacement technology was powerful, but it was also flawed. There were so many variables to account for, so many things that could go devastatingly wrong.

But there were so many things that could go right, too.

If you were careful.

So careful the Admiral was as he took a step toward the Commander and angled his head up.

The planet around them was nothing more than a barren wasteland, just so much dead pockmarked rock and rolling gray hills.

It was a suitable backdrop as the red light of the adjustment beam pulsed so brightly around the Commander, it could have been mistaken for a new sun taking form.

The Admiral waited. One more second. Then he stepped forward and opened his arms wide, almost as if he were accepting a long-lost friend.

The beam pulsed around him, growing up his arms and snapping around his head like greedy tentacles getting ready to drag him down to some impenetrable depth.

The Admiral didn't scream. Not a single breath, in fact. He felt pain, though. True, hard, deep – the feel of a man who was being ripped apart from the inside out.

But the feeling didn't last.

Just as the Admiral's consciousness felt as if it could take no more, he felt himself shift.

His body crumpled beneath him, but his mind – ah, his mind spread. It felt like someone had taken his awareness, applied it to a knife, and spread it across reality like a generous serving of butter.

The next thing he knew, he was smeared right over the Commander.

The man was still suspended there in that ball of pulsing red light.

His helmet had been forced to recede, and now there was nothing to stop the Admiral from staring right into the Commander's eyes.

The Commander was afraid. The Admiral wondered if the man had ever felt fear on a scale like this before.

No matter. One thing was certain – even if the Commander hadn't felt fear like this before, he would feel fear like this – and much worse – soon.

For as the Admiral's consciousness was spread toward the Commander, the Admiral took over, never to be pushed back again. Though it might take some time for the Admiral to gain full control over the Commander's body, it was a battle the Commander had no hope of ultimately winning. It would simply be a matter of time before the Admiral took what was his and finally ended this.

The light suddenly cut out. No warning. Nothing.

No sound, either.

The Commander's body dropped. Though it was limp, somehow, the Commander shifted at the last moment and landed on one knee with one hand pressed into the dusty ground below him.

... It took several long seconds until he moved again. His body was rigid, like carved steel.

Then, finally, with the creak of joint and muscle, he tilted his head up.

He stood.

And he walked toward the stone palace.

Chapter Three

Leana'x

She sat there in the center of the room, her body crumpled in on itself as she hooked her arms around her legs with all her might.

She was no longer rocking back and forth – couldn't spare the energy. All she could do was sit there and not look at the screens.

... They felt like they were connected to her. But not in a positive way. No. It felt like they were somehow sapping her energy.

But there was a problem – she needed her energy. For with every second it was taken away from her... she felt thin, like someone was buffing her away.

She felt something oozing out of her nostril, and a second later, there was the faintest sound as a single droplet of blue blood splashed against her knee.

She jerked her head up and stared at it, finally unhooking her arms, bringing up a shaking finger, and touching it to the blood.

It was still warm, but only barely.

... This couldn't just be the fatigue and pain of her fights.

Leana'x could... she could swear something was happening to her.

Suddenly, the screen on the opposite side of the room shifted. No warning. In a second, it went from being hooked against the wall to zooming forward and coming to a stop right in front of her nose.

She screamed and jerked backward, trying to scuttle back before the screen could squash her flat. But it didn't ram into her and pin her against the wall. It stopped just an inch in front of her nose. So much light spilled off it and lit up her face, it felt like she was staring down the barrel of a laser gun.

She inched backward, but the screen followed her.

It wasn't a hologram – wasn't just made of collected light.

It was solid. And it was floating, without a noise.

She brought up a shaking hand.

The screen seemed to react, and followed her move, shifting as her hand did.

"I'm... controlling this?" she said to no one in particular.

Something answered. In clipped clear tones. But there was a problem. It wasn't in the Standard Galactic Tongue. It wasn't even in old Artaxan.

It was in a language she'd never heard before.

Maybe the electronic voice expected an answer, but when she didn't give one, the screen shifted toward her once more, an insistent quality to the movement.

She didn't throw herself backward like she'd be squashed this time; she simply stared at it warily as the voice repeated.

"I'm sorry, I don't know what you're saying. I don't speak your language," she tried.

The voice repeated its message yet again.

"I don't know what you're saying!" Leana'x said again, the words quicker with emotion and frustration as a new wave of tears slicked her cheeks, trailed over her chin, and splashed against the torn, dust-covered fabric of her collar.

The voice repeated once more, and the screen got closer yet again.

Though the screen was on, she had no idea whatsoever what it was depicting. It could have been intel, or maybe live telemetry from some part of the moon or the palace, but she couldn't tell. She simply didn't understand the symbols, no matter how far she stretched her memory.

The voice repeated.

Leana'x began to sob louder. She also brought up her hand, curled it into a defeated fist, and struck it against the ground. Or at least, she tried to. Just at the last moment, she felt something reach out of the screen.

It happened in a snapped second – one her already tired mind couldn't keep up with.

But there was no denying her senses as a blue hand made out of light stretched out of the screen and locked around her wrist.

Though Leana'x tried to shift back, the hand remained locked on her wrist, and she simply pulled it further out of the screen.

The next thing she knew, a full figure had formed, stepping out of the screen and looming over Leana'x.

Leana'x, now practically on her back as she stared up, dumbfounded, couldn't say a word.

The figure looked like they were a hologram. They were blue and made of light, and yet, it was a light wholly different to the usual holograms she'd seen. Not just the standard holograms of the Coalition, but the more advanced light tech of her people too.

No. Whatever the hell this thing was in front of her, she had no experience with it whatsoever.

The figure resembled a female member of Leana'x's race – without the blue skin, at least. From her thick green hair to her eyes, she resembled Artaxans. Even her movements were familiar as the hologram tilted her head to the side and stared at Leana'x.

"... Who are you? What do you want? Where did you come from?"

The figure didn't answer.

That would be when Leana'x caught sight of her eyes. They weren't like the ordinary eyes of an Artaxan. Instead, even from her position at the figure's feet, Leana'x could see there were tiny little cogs and wheels of light within the woman's retinas. They shifted this way and that, as if they were assessing Leana'x somehow.

The woman spoke. But it was in the same unknown language Leana'x had no hope of understanding.

Leana'x just sat there staring up at the woman, with no idea what to do.

The woman continued to tilt her head to the side, and as Leana'x looked up, she could see the woman's eyes were still twisting around as those cogs of light moved like tiny machines.

... Were they some form of scanner? It wasn't as crazy as it sounded, because Leana'x swore she could feel something penetrating her, accessing her body somehow.

It took a second for her to realize what that was.

AVA.

Leana'x still couldn't access AVA no matter how much

she wanted to. For if only she could access AVA, the artificial intelligence would be able to tell Leana'x what to do, how to control this palace, how to save John.

At the mere thought of John, even though Leana'x thought she'd already felt the worst of her grief, her heart felt like someone had squashed it.

She even brought up a hand and crumpled it on her chest.

That would be when the woman finally reacted. Her pupils widened with an emotion that looked a heck of a lot like fear, and she leaned forward.

Leana'x didn't have the time to buck back as the light woman reached forward and locked a hand on Leana'x's forehead.

It was hot, and there was a shifting kind of feeling, as if the woman's hand was made up of vibrating particles. Which it probably was.

Leana'x stared up at the woman, her eyes open wide.

... It was almost like the woman was checking Leana'x's temperature. And when she shifted back quickly, a worried look on her face, it was clear the woman didn't like what she found.

Without any warning whatsoever, the hologram shifted forward and picked Leana'x up.

Leana'x spluttered and jerked, but there was nothing she could do. Not only was she weak, but the woman was made of light, goddamn it. There was nothing for Leana'x to fight.

Still, Leana'x wasn't going to make this easy. She tried to buck and jerk off the hologram's shoulder.

That would be when the woman cracked her lips open and said, "Still."

Leana'x stopped dead.

... The hologram spoke Standard Galactic Tongue after all?

"Learning language. Speak more," the hologram instructed.

Leana'x's head reeled. Her thoughts felt as if they'd been fed into a blender, and she'd never have a hope of making sense of them again.

The woman strode over and reached the door, shoving a hand forward and elegantly swiping it to the side.

It riveted Leana'x's attention on the woman's fingers. They were heavily decorated with tattoos. Except they weren't just tattoos. As Leana'x stared, she saw the little black symbols dart around, almost as if they too were live telemetry.

It took Leana'x's breath away. She didn't have time to think about how underequipped she'd been for this palace; she just let out a breathy hiss. "What are you?"

"Living knowledge of palace. Speak more. Will learn."

The last thing Leana'x wanted to do was speak. She wanted to curl in on herself and cry her heart out until John came back.

... But John wasn't coming back. There was no way he would have been able to hold the Admiral back, let alone defeat the man.

Just as dread and grief swept around her like a hurricane, the woman stopped and inclined her head over her shoulder, her electronic eyes locking on Leana'x. "Safe. Be safe. Can't die."

Leana'x shivered. The hologram was obviously continually scanning Leana'x's bio readings, and it was just as obvious that the woman didn't like what she saw.

Leana'x swallowed. "How sick am I?"

"Dying. Need help. Will give it. Speak so I will learn," the hologram said.

Leana'x stopped. Her head felt numb all of a sudden, as if she'd shoved her brains in a transporter and sent them to an ice planet.

... Leana'x was dying? That was... that was the reason blood was still dripping out of her nose, wasn't it? That was the reason she could no longer access AVA properly.

"Don't fear. Fear undermines, makes sicker. Strong. Stay strong," the woman said.

Strong? How in hell was Leana'x meant to stay strong when everything she knew and loved had been taken away from her?

Leana'x had a secret, and it was one that everyone could see. She wasn't someone who connected with people easily. Sure, she had a few friends, but she could easily count them on one hand. And even then, the interactions she had with them would never reach too deep. Because she never let anyone in that deep.

Maybe it was on account of her heritage, or maybe even without her title, Leana'x would have always been a cold and distant person.

But none of that was the point. The point was that right now Leana'x was feeling loss like she'd never felt it before. Because, without being aware of it, she had started to connect.

To John. The guy who'd once turned her life into a living hell. But the guy who'd now been taken away from her forever.

... More blood slipped from her nose and trickled onto the woman's shoulder. As soon as it touched the hologram's apparent skin, it sizzled and evaporated.

The woman stopped. She inclined her head even

further over her shoulder, now locking her full gaze on Leana'x, the hologram's electronic eyes narrowing, the cogs spinning faster. "Whatever you think, stop thinking it. Hurting you. Can't afford more damage. Damage lead to sooner death."

It was such a cold way to put it. Worse, not only was Leana'x in this position, now she couldn't even afford to grieve.

Just when she wanted to pull even further into her sorrow and just turn numb, the woman finally opened the door and walked out into the corridor. Except it was different to the corridor Leana'x had left when she'd entered this room. It was much wider. It also seemed to be high up a tower. She saw a glimpse from a simple window that seemed to show an unrivaled view of the naked, barren wasteland of the moon below.

Leana'x instantly tried to jerk toward it, even though she had no hope of pulling herself off the shoulder of the woman. Leana'x opened her eyes as wide as they could possibly go as she tried to catch a glimpse of John... or whatever was left of him. Something, anything to give her a sense of closure.

The woman stopped. "Why strain toward the outside?" she said haltingly.

"John," Leana'x managed, her voice so choked, an ordinary person wouldn't be able to pick it up. "The Commander," she added. "My..." she trailed off, incapable of finishing the thought as hot tears streaked down her cheeks and dashed against her collar.

"John? The Commander? Who?"

"I... I traveled here with him. He protected me from the various people trying to assassinate me. He... he helped me..." she defaulted to saying. What she really wanted to say was he'd died for her, and it was tearing her up inside. If John had never met Leana'x, he'd still be safe aboard his ship.

Leana'x should never have left the home world.

"Withdrawing inside. Thinking. Stop. No more thoughts. Speak. So that I can understand."

Leana'x didn't bother to point out that to speak, one needed to think. She just felt the grief slam into her again as the hologram finally shifted past the window and continued to walk down the open corridor.

Though the last thing Leana'x wanted to do was be drawn in by this place, she couldn't stop her curiosity as it welled within her.

Wherever they were in the palace, it felt different to the lower levels. It... felt more sophisticated, more intelligent somehow. Yeah, Leana'x could appreciate that didn't make any sense. Because buildings, no matter how sophisticated, were not intelligent creatures. They weren't creatures, full stop. They were structures made out of inanimate matter.

... so why did this place feel like it was somehow alive?

"Speak," the hologram commanded again.

Leana'x had no idea what to say, so she said the first thing that popped into her head. "What are you? What's your name?" she added, as if that was somehow the most important fact she could learn.

"I am Na'van. I am Light Guard."

"... Light Guard? What's that?"

"Original protectors of Gift."

At the mere mention of this gift, Leana'x's back straightened as if she'd been struck, and a race of tingles slammed hard down her stomach. "What... what gift?"

"Intelligence," Na'van answered.

... Leana'x stopped. Not that she was moving or

anything. But her feelings stopped for a single second, her thoughts too.

AVA. Na'van was clearly talking about AVA.

At the prospect that Na'van knew anything about AVA, Leana'x opened her mouth to demand some answers, but she stopped.

Abruptly. Because she couldn't afford for this to be a trap. AVA was the most important secret Leana'x had right now. And even if she was forced to shoulder this incredible burden on her own now that John was dead, she couldn't give up.

"You pause. Suspicion. No need. I know you are her."

Again, Leana'x's back pulsed with nerves. Hard and hot, they were the kind of tingles that felt as if they'd pull her skin apart. "Her?"

"AVA," Na'van said, and for the first time, there was an elegance about her voice, not just her movements as she continued to gracefully and easily heft Leana'x down the corridor.

"... You know about AVA?"

"You are the new Prime. You are the new AVA," Na'van answered smoothly.

Leana'x shook her head, despite the fact the move was unnecessary and costly. "I'm not AVA.... I just carry her."

"You are now AVA. But not whole," Na'van pointed out as she narrowed her eyes at Leana'x.

Leana'x blinked hard, a few tears welling behind her eyes. "No... when AVA inhabited my body... there was a man present. John."

"The man who haunts you now," Na'van said, her standard tongue getting better with every sentence.

Leana'x hadn't used the word haunted, and she had no idea how Na'van had learned it, but it was apt.

Because John was haunting Leana'x, body and soul.

A few more tears leaked out of her eyes, but she didn't bother to dry them. "Yeah... the guy who haunts me. He... died. Someone attacked him outside. An Admiral from the Coalition," she continued to explain, even though Na'van would have no way of knowing what the heck she was talking about.

"You mean a Replacement," Na'van said.

"How do you know that?"

"I have already scanned your immediate memories."

"*What*? How?"

"I accessed the specific region of your brain that allows communication through thought waves," Na'van revealed as she continued to stride down the corridor.

Leana'x had no idea where Na'van was taking her, but that wasn't nearly as important as what Na'van had just revealed. "You... you've been reading my mind?"

"I have been accessing your recent thoughts, yes. It is allowing me to understand. This situation is critical. We must stabilize you now before going out to retrieve the other connection to AVA."

It took Leana'x a moment, a moment where her brain struggled to catch up and her head hurt. But she pushed through it.

She blinked. "Wait... what do you mean retrieve the other connection to AVA? Do you mean... John's body?"

"I mean the man you call John. He's still alive."

Leana'x couldn't think. In that moment, she felt herself stretch away.

Then she snapped back as she curled harder around Na'van's shoulders. "What do you mean John's still alive? You... are you somehow connected to the outside of this palace?"

"I am wired into the scanners of this palace, correct. They continuously scan the moon for any new data. I have a lock on the man you call John. He was attacked by a Replacement. The Replacement contained him in some kind of radiation – one our scanners do not recognize."

Leana'x was practically choking. She felt as if she'd never breathe again. But she managed to break her lips open and hiss, "So he's alive? He got free? He killed the Admiral?"

"The Admiral appeared to die on his own."

Leana'x didn't bother to point out that that made no damn sense. She just began to sob.

But the tears of joy didn't last. She started to buck again.

"What are you doing?"

"Put me down. Put me down. I have to go out and get John."

"You can't leave this palace. To do so would put your already taxed body under too much strain. Estimated time until you die would be 5 minutes and 38 seconds."

That was a truly sickening thought and should have made Leana'x wonder just how much time she had left in general, but she couldn't think about that right now.

She continued to struggle. "I have to go save John. He's connected to AVA," she tried, hoping that any appeal to the Intelligence would force Na'van to stop.

"We are aware of this. Just as we're aware of the fact that he is not at death's door – a term I have picked up from your mind."

"I know what death's door is. And I'm fine. We have to—"

Na'van took a hard turn to the side, and a section of the wall suddenly fell away to reveal a room within.

Unlike all the other rooms and corridors of this palace she'd seen so far, this room looked modern.

It felt... god, it felt alive, too.

As soon as Na'van strode in through the door, Leana'x reeled.

There was such a spinning pressure in her head, she wanted to pitch to her knees and throw up.

Again, Na'van wouldn't let her.

She strode straight toward a pod on the opposite wall. Leana'x could just see it through her suddenly bleary vision.

The pod was connected to the very wall with... Leana'x had to lean closer to see it.

Was it hair? No. It just resembled the same hair Leana'x now had as the Prime.

"... What is that stuff?"

"Living matter. It connects this palace to you. Or will. The palace will help bolster your body until it can be healed."

"Wait. Just wait," Leana'x said as Na'van took her over to the pod.

Na'van got down on one knee in front of it, and with no effort at all, lifted Leana'x into it.

Leana'x was way beyond struggling. Just entering the room had done something to her, sapping even more of her energy.

She felt like her consciousness was a black hole that was about to suck the rest of her into it.

She managed to open one eye and lock it onto Na'van as she stood above her.

"You... you need to save John. Please, save John. He has AVA... and I can't do this without him."

Na'van didn't answer. Or maybe she did, but Leana'x's mind shut down before she could hear it.

The lights went out. Blackness swamped Leana'x's vision, and as it did, she heard a click as the pod shut.

Relief filled her.

Then she lost consciousness.

The question would be whether she would wake up.

Chapter Four

Commander Campbell

He stood there shaking his head, trying to make sense of what happened to him.

And, more importantly, what happened to the damn Admiral.

John stood above the Admiral, and for what felt like the tenth time, John took a step forward and poked the Admiral's boot with his own.

The Admiral's head flopped further to the side, but it wasn't a voluntary move and it sure as hell wasn't a prelude to an attack. It was just the movement from John kicking his foot.

The guy was dead. John didn't even need his armor's scanners to confirm that. His skin was falling away from him in dirty chunks, like he was turning to ash and rotting before John's very eyes.

John stood there and stared for a few more seconds until he finally took a step backward. His legs were jerky, and his armor didn't react as smoothly as it should.

... That would be on account of whatever the hell had happened to John. When that red light had swamped him, he'd thought he would be torn to shreds. He'd felt it happening, too. This godawful sensation that he couldn't even begin to describe. It was as if that red light had spread into his body with the explicit purpose of splitting every one of his cells in half.

... Including his mind.

That thought slammed into his head from somewhere. It caused him to jerk to the side and bring a hand up to his head.

His visor was still off. Fortunately, his shield had snapped into place. It didn't rebuff his armored fingers as the shield recognized them and let them through. He pushed his hand against his brow, scratching it as if I was looking for a way in.

But He didn't find a way in, because there wasn't a goddamn hole in his head.

He took another step back from the Admiral. There was no reason for John to be hovering over his body. Though John's armor and body had been put through hell with that red light, according to John's armor's onboard sensors, it hadn't done any lasting damage.

In other words, the Admiral was dead, John was fine, and he really had to pull himself away and get to Leana'x already.

Just the thought of her was enough to finally see John turn around. As he did, he cast my gaze upward. He sought out a glimpse of the Admiral's ship.

After he'd died and the red light had stopped trying to tear John in half, the prototype ship had shot off into space. For a while, John had feared it was just getting vantage for a better shot to obliterate him. But now enough time had passed that John was relatively confident that it wasn't coming back.

Maybe it had been programmed to leave the moon if its master died and return to Artaxan Prime.

Or maybe it was just holding pattern in orbit – didn't matter.

John did what he should have done the second he'd been released from that red light – he turned on his heel to run for the palace.

He threw himself across the pockmarked gray ground, running as fast as his armor would allow.

Though he was sure it hadn't been damaged, it also... didn't feel right. Or maybe that was just his skin.

It itched. Kind of throbbed a bit. It almost... Christ, though it sounded crazy, it almost sounded as if his skin was trying to stretch around another body.

It would be the armor. Must be a slight malfunction. He'd take it off and look at it as soon as he confirmed she was alright.

He ran as fast as he goddamn could until he finally reached the rise and threw himself down it.

He came to a skidding stop in front of a stone palace.

It looked... like a ruin. No, that wasn't the right term – because it wasn't actually in ruins.

It was squat and had many rooms, but it was technically whole. It was just extremely basic considering the structures John was used to. This was no incredible tower on Artaxan Prime. This was just so much carved stone.

Though John wanted to run until he found her, he wasn't stupid enough to throw himself at the palace.

Leana'x had already warned him about the fact the palace was programmed to only allow Artaxans in. Though there was a fair chance that John would now be recognized as an Artaxan, he still needed to take it carefully, no matter what his heart wanted to do.

So he slowed right down, brought up both of his gauntlets, and spread the fingers wide as he tried to scan the palace.

... If he could believe the telemetry coming in on his visor, then the palace was literally just stone.

... But that would be when something blipped.

John's brow dropped down low. "What the hell?" he began, paying so much attention to the telemetry coming over his visor that he forgot to just use his eyes.

Then he saw something move out of the corner of his vision.

A woman, to be precise. He didn't give his heart the chance to thump with hope, to beat right out of his chest and reach toward Leana'x. Because it wasn't her.

As John let his hands drop, he saw a naked blue woman who resembled Artaxans, and yet, didn't at the same time.

There was a covered courtyard that ran around the front of the palace. The woman walked right up to it but stopped just before her body could venture beyond the building.

She looked at him.

He looked back.

Shit. Leana'x had told him this place was abandoned.

He opened his mouth.

She gestured forward. No words. No introduction. She just turned on her foot gracefully and walked back into the palace.

Though John knew he should be careful here, screw being careful. "Hey, what's going on? Hey? Have you seen Leana'x?" He ran forward, despite the fact a man as trained as he should have hung back to figure out what he was facing.

John couldn't think right now. And it wasn't just at the prospect of finding Leana'x. It was... he couldn't put his finger on it. It was almost as if his own head had become an inhospitable place for his own thoughts.

Crazy.

It would just be the stress. The fight. The light. Some combination.

He just had to get to her.

He ran past the threshold of the palace before he really appreciated what he was doing. He wasn't struck down, though, just sailed right through.

He stopped several meters into the courtyard, turned around, looked up, then focused back on the woman. She'd stopped several meters ahead. Again she looked at him and waved forward.

"Wait. Who are you? What is this place? Where's Leana'x?"

"She is in stasis," the woman answered in the Standard Galactic Tongue, even though her words and accent were halting, as if she'd just learned how to speak.

John paled. "Wait? What? What the hell do you mean she's in stasis? What happened to her?"

"She is breaking apart."

John ground to a stop, fear barreling into him from every angle like an army. "What?" he choked.

"No body is designed to hold the Gift without assistance."

"... You mean AVA?"

"Yes. The Gift from the Originals. Nobody – not even the engineered Artaxans – can hold AVA without help.

There is help in this palace." The woman turned back around and continued to lead John forward.

John threw himself at her, his heart pounding in his chest.

Though he barely had the time to appreciate this, his fear at what was happening to Leana'x was doing one thing. It was pushing back that godawful fog in his mind – the very fog that told him he didn't belong in his own head anymore.

A fog that was threatening to settle further into his body with every step.

But John pushed it away and concentrated on following the woman.

Leana'x... she'd better be okay. And if she wasn't, John would move the goddamn galaxy to save her.

Chapter Five

Admiral Jones

He was fighting. Trying with every second to take over the Commander's brain.

But it wasn't easy. Because every time that fool felt another wave of emotion, it disrupted Jones' growing control.

But the Admiral had no intention of giving up. The Commander would make a mistake, sooner rather than later, letting go of his mental defenses long enough for the Admiral to finally sweep in.

The hologram woman continued to lead the Commander down the hall.

The Admiral had never seen tech like her before. At least, the side of him that remembered the real Admiral Jones' knowledge hadn't seen anything like it. The Force had seen her kind before.

Light Guards.

Remnant soldiers from the Originals who were meant

to protect the Artaxans and their secret. The Admiral was surprised any were still alive.

Obviously this palace had been holding onto one for eons.

... The presence of the Light Guard meant one thing – the Admiral would have to bide his time before he killed the Prime. Though his greed wanted to see him snap in and strangle that woman's neck, he would have to wait. All he would need was for the Light Guard to leave the room and for the idiot Commander to have a single moment of weakness, and this would end.

Then AVA would inhabit this body – the Admiral was sure of it. For now the Admiral had made his way into the Commander's mind, he could appreciate just how much AVA had changed him. Not just the Commander's armor, mind you – but the man's very brain. The mere act of communicating with the Intelligence had changed Commander Campbell's body at the genetic level.

And without those changes, the Admiral wouldn't have been able to infect the man.

If the Admiral could have smiled, he would have.

Instead, he bided his time for the opportunity that would soon come....

...

Prince Maqx

It was a gamble, but he was prepared for that.

He'd left the vault far behind. He was now in the primary communication hub of the Prime Palace.

Beyond the windows that swept around one whole side of the room, he saw Artaxan Prime.

There were ships holding in a defensive position

around the palace, incapable of penetrating beyond the shields that protected the place.

The Prince almost wanted to bring a hand up and wave at them. There was no point, though – as they wouldn't be able to see in through the windows, even though they were ostensibly clear.

No scanners would be able to penetrate the building. In other words, no one would know what he was doing.

The Prince leaned in front of the primary communications panel. In front of it, he practically held the communications of the Coalition in his palm. The Artaxans were connected to everyone, and with a single click of a single button, the Prince could send a message across the Milky Way.

He didn't pause. With his eyes locked on the ships retaining their holding pattern beyond, he let his fingers fly across the panel.

The Admiral had been a fool. There was a better way of going after Leana'x. A much smarter way.

Why blaze across the galaxy desperately trying to kill her, when all the Prince had to do was wait for the galaxy to deliver her to his doorstep?

The galaxy thought it knew what had happened to every other member of the Artaxan Royal Family, apart from Leana'x. Well, now the Prince was going to write them a new version of that story.

"You were a fool, Admiral Jones," the Prince muttered to himself as his fingers continued to fly across the panel in front of him. "And now this is up to me."

The Admiral wasn't dead. Not completely. He had been severely injured, though. At least, the Prince believed that was what had happened. He couldn't make full sense of what had occurred to the Admiral's biological readings.

They'd certainly changed, though, weakening immeasurably.

And that was enough for the Prince to finally take hold.

He smiled at the ships and waved once more as he sent them, and everyone else, a message. Or was it an ultimatum?

Perhaps it was both.

Chapter Six

Commander Campbell

His head was pounding, but he ignored it.

The woman finally stopped in front of a room, spread her hand to the side, and walked in as a door opened.

John threw himself in behind her.

He should really be more careful around this woman – he knew that. His training kept repeating it to him, too, but he couldn't shake the feeling that she wasn't a threat.

She seemed to be a fixture of the palace, if that made any sense.

... He almost felt connected to her, too.

Or maybe he was making that up.

This room was large and stuffed with so much tech he didn't recognize, he should have set his scanners to take up as much data as he could.

He didn't. As the woman moved to the side, John finally saw her.

"Leana'x," he said, the word like a hand reaching out of his throat to find her.

He rushed over.

She was in some kind of pod that was attached to the wall with glowing string that looked almost exactly like her hair.

He could just see Leana'x through the glass window of her otherwise sleek white metal pod.

Though he wanted to bring up a hand and knock on the pod, the woman immediately stepped in and grabbed his hand, holding it firmly in place. "Do not interfere with the pod. It is keeping her alive."

John felt like he'd just been punched in the gut. He had to swallow past a dry throat. "What do you mean it's keeping her alive? What happened to her?"

"Her body is not designed to hold AVA without technical assistance. Such assistance resides in the primary palace room on Artaxan Prime. Though the Prime can leave that room, it is not recommended to leave it for long stretches of time. To do so will slowly kill the Prime."

John felt like the woman kept punching him, even though all she was doing was speaking.

He just didn't want to take this in. It seemed that every time he had something to cheer about, he was promptly knocked down again.

He somehow defeated the Admiral, only to find that Leana'x was....

The woman took a step back, shot him a warning look, and let go of his hand. Then she looked right at him.

Though John didn't want to tear his gaze from Leana'x, he had no option as the woman stared right at him. He caught sight of her eyes. They weren't biological. They were... like these tiny moving cogs made out of light.

He swallowed again. "... What are you?"

"I am a Light Guard. I belong to this palace. I am a remnant from the Originals, kept to protect the Gift."

"... So you know about AVA? Does that mean you know how to save Leana'x?" John's mind jumped from thought to thought and emotion to emotion.

The emotion seemed to be the key, because the more of it he felt, the more centered in his body he became. It was as if his pounding heart was the only thing keeping him in his body, like a single rope mooring a large vessel to shore.

"She must remain in the pod until her body can begin the healing process. It will buy her the time she needs. But she must be transported back to Artaxan Prime. Once she leaves this pod, she will have 2 days. If she does not reach the throne room in that time, she will break."

John didn't react.

He should. He should freak out at what she was saying.

... So why did he want to smile? Why could he feel his goddamn lips trying to curl as if this horrendous news was the best thing he'd ever heard?

That thought horrified him so much, he tuned out as the woman continued to explain things.

... It... it took him a hell of a long time to shake his head and dispel whatever had just happened to his body. Whatever sick thoughts had insinuated their way into his mind.

"Wait... what did you just say?" he managed.

"Leana'x will have to stay in that pod for the next 12 hours. Then she will have exactly 2 days to make it to the throne room. Only the technology present in the throne room will be able to heal her fully."

John took a breath. He brought a hand up and pressed it through the shield of his armor, locking it against his head. "There's no way we can make it to Artaxan Prime in that time."

"I will alter your vessel, ensuring it can make the trip."

John looked at her. His... eyes were narrowed for some reason. As if the prospect that this woman could alter his ship was far more interesting than the fact it would allow John to save Leana'x in time.

He brought a hand up and wiped his suddenly sweaty mouth. "... Will it work?"

"Yes," she said flatly.

"... Good. But, wait – no. No one's been able to get into the palace on Artaxan Prime since the mass assassination. Wait – do you even know about the assassination?" he kept speaking back on himself. He just couldn't think straight....

"I am a Light Guard. I possess the ability to gain information from multiple sources. I know of these things," the Light Guard said.

John should have probably bothered to ask how she'd learned about this stuff, but he couldn't focus on more than one thing at the moment.

He kept his hand locked on his mouth as he breathed harder. Then he looked past the Light Guard, right at Leana'x.

As soon as he locked his eyes on her through the glass window, his stomach kicked and twisted.

... She wasn't moving in there. Yeah, he knew how stasis tech worked. He knew she was still alive. But you tell that to his catapulting heart.

The blue hologram kept her eyes on him as he leaned closer to the pod, and it was clear that if he made any hasty moves, she'd wrench him back.

So he just stared at Leana'x and finally pulled himself away.

He still didn't know if he could trust this woman, but there was nothing telling him he couldn't, either.

He forced himself to straighten as he stared at the hologram directly. "You said you were a Light Guard, what is that?"

"We have been retained from the original times for the explicit purpose of ensuring the Gift does not fall into the hands of the Force."

John didn't let himself react. Which was hard.

At the mention of the Force, usually, his stomach wanted to race right out of his damn body and flee the friggin' Milky Way.

Usually.

... So why... why did he feel almost a rush of anticipation at the mere mention of their name this time? Why did his heart soar as if the Force spilling into this galaxy would be the most welcome thing that could possibly happen?

John settled for taking a hard swallow and forcing himself to pay attention as it sank through his throat and down into his chest.

The Light Guard's eyes were on him, always focusing in and out like little targeting lasers on the end of a long-range gun. "You appear to be uncomfortable at the mention of the Force. Do you not know what they are?"

John pushed his peculiar reaction well and truly away as he shook his head. "I'm aware of what they are. Just as I'm aware of their... sheer destructive capacity. I... I'm just a little..." he trailed off as he shook his head hard. He dropped his gaze and locked it on Leana'x again. He thought just by staring at her that it would calm his mind. But he felt it again – this rising tide of something climbing through his body, almost trying to get to his brain.

He shook his head and took a forced step back, the hologram's eyes on him the entire time.

"What happened to you outside the palace when that Replacement attacked you?" the Light Guard said.

John didn't answer right away.

Not because he had anything to hide. It was just....

He inclined his head far to the side, brought up a hand, and pressed it over his brow.

"What's the problem?" the Light Guard asked.

"I... I can't really remember the fight clearly anymore. I don't even know why Admiral Jones died."

"While the sensors in this palace could not pick up the origin nor nature of the weapon the Admiral used to attack you, I can assure you that Replacement technology is flawed. Even back in the days of the Original War with the Force and the founders of the Milky Way, Replacement technology was deeply defective. Now, with the intervening countless millennia, the technology would have only become more damaged. The Admiral may very well have died due to a critical deformation in one of his organs."

As the Light Guard spoke, her words kind of flowed past John, as if he'd reverted to a baby and couldn't comprehend language anymore.

It took him so long to shake his head. He opened his mouth, too, ready to tell her that was a hell of an assumption.

But he stopped.

Right there, with his mouth half open and the reply readying on his lips, his voice just froze.

All of its own accord.

... Why the hell did it feel as if he wasn't in control of his own body anymore?

"As for the technology that was used to immobilize you, though the palace sensors were incapable of getting a clear reading on it, your Coalition armor would have. If you agree to upload its data to our systems—"

"No," John found himself saying. His tone was hard, his voice forthright.

The Light Guard looked confused. "Though we are not technically part of the Coalition, we fall under the Artaxan Protectorate. In sharing this information with us, you will not be violating—"

"It's not going to happen," John said again. Except was it really him saying it?

Jesus Christ, he just didn't know what was happening to his body. It was like there was another damn person living in his mind.

He took a step back from the Light Guard, then another as he locked a hand over his mouth as if he was scared of the damn thing talking without his permission again. "Look, first things first – you need to make the alterations to our ship that you talked about," John forced himself to say, and once the words were out, he could appreciate their wisdom.

What had happened to John was one thing, but their biggest priority by far at the moment had to be Leana'x and AVA. And if this Light Guard wasn't lying to John, and Leana'x would have precisely two days to make it to the throne room, then they had to figure out how to do that now.

John took a far stronger and more coordinated step backward, and he inclined his head upward. "I'll call the ship down from orbit and park it wherever you want. Then you can make the changes to its propulsion drives as I watch over Leana'x."

His voice was even.

... His mind wasn't.

Leana'x didn't need watching over, and right now, he

should be contacting the Coalition to figure out how they were going to get to Artaxan Prime, let alone into the throne room. The last John had heard, the palace was still locked down, presumably by the same force that perpetrated the mass assassination.

Even with a faster ship, it was still going to be almost impossible to get Leana'x into the throne room in time.

... And yet, instead of offering to do the sensible thing and calling the Coalition, John had offered to stand here and protect Leana'x.

From what?

The Light Guard didn't immediately take him up on his offer, vacate the room, and leave him alone with Leana'x. She just watched John with those electronic eyes of hers. "The Prime will need no guarding. There is no one else in this palace apart from you, her, and myself. I will require your assistance in altering your vessel. Though I was proficient in all forms of known technology once upon a time, those times have changed. I will be able to adapt and learn quickly, but I will need your guidance."

This was where John should nod and accept her offer.

That's what his training told him to do, what mere decency and common sense confirmed he should do, too. So why did he let his gaze flick toward Leana'x in the pod once more? Wait, no – his gaze didn't flick; it sliced.

He could feel the Light Guard's attention on him again.

John realized he couldn't just stand here and stare at Leana'x like that, so he finally forced himself to take a step backward, then another.

He looked the Light Guard right in the eye and nodded.

But the move was stiff. Heck, everything about John was stiff.

He knew he needed some kind of medical intervention

– a thorough scan of some description, just to ensure that whatever had happened with the Admiral hadn't permanently affected him.

Yeah, John knew that – but for some reason he didn't act on that knowledge. He just whirled on his foot and followed the Light Guard out of the room. But not before turning over his shoulder and shooting Leana'x a long look in her pod. His eyes didn't tick over her face, and nor were they drawn in by her still, serene expression.

No. They locked on her throat, as if the only thing Commander John Campbell wanted to do right now was clutch his hands around her neck and squeeze.

He tried to shake that off.

He couldn't.

So he followed.

Chapter Seven

Admiral Jones

He was biding his time.

But that time wasn't coming nearly as quickly enough as he'd hoped.

The fool John Campbell was proving harder to control than the Admiral would have liked.

But time would tell who would become the ultimate victor over this body. And as the Commander didn't even know he was in a fight for his life, the advantage was firmly with the Admiral.

An ordinary mind wouldn't have the capacity to understand the realm he was now in. An ordinary mind was used to being stuck in an ordinary body.

But a Replacement's mind was anything but ordinary.

Though the Replacement technology hadn't been built for this specific purpose, it had adapted perfectly.

The Admiral was struck by the fact he was the only person in the entire Milky Way who could have completed this task. No other creature, even from the advanced psychic races, would have the wherewithal to reach inside another's mind and attempt to take it over from the inside out.

It was like fighting a purely conceptual battle. No players, no pieces, no weapons – other than his own thoughts.

And his thoughts kept focusing on wrapping his hands around Leana'x's throat.

The wretched Light Guard strode ahead through the stone corridors of the palace, never turning over her shoulder to look at the Commander. But that didn't matter. Even if the Commander himself wasn't aware of it, Admiral Jones knew the Light Guard would be keeping a permanent scanner lock on the Commander.

But the question was did the Light Guard suspect anything?

One thing was clear – she was being honest. If she'd suspected what that red light was that had encapsulated the Commander, the Light Guard would have already attacked.

But she was allowing the Commander almost free rein through the palace, which meant she had no clue.

No clue at all.

Admiral Jones would have smiled if he could. But there was no point in making the Commander even more suspicious, simply to control his lips for a fraction of a second.

No, bide your time, the Admiral thought to himself.

The opportunity he was waiting for would come sooner rather than later.

The Light Guard led the Commander through the palace until they reached an open courtyard in the center.

Though the Admiral was too busy constantly prying and poking at the Commander's mind to try to find a permanent doorway into the man's consciousness, the Admiral could still appreciate one thing. This courtyard felt strange. Even the Commander, with his primitive body and armor, could appreciate that as he suddenly shivered, grabbed his arms, and tried to chase the sensation away.

"... What is this place?" the Commander asked as he looked around the open space.

The stone palace looked like nothing more than an old, basic structure you would get on a technologically impoverished world. But the feel of it was completely other.

John's body was having a visceral reaction to it, which was bad. As every time John's attention was brought back to his beating heart, panting lungs, or shaking limbs, the Admiral's control slipped.

"This is where you will land your ship," the Light Guard said.

The Admiral could feel John frown. "Why does it feel... I can't put my finger on it," the Commander managed ineloquently.

"There is invisible technology beneath the ground. It comes from the Originals. The bridge you formed between your consciousness and AVA's, though it is technically no longer functioning as Leana'x is in stasis, would have still altered you sufficiently to be able to recognize this place on a physical level."

The Commander forced a deep breath into his lungs.

Though Admiral Jones was technically inside Campbell's mind, he wasn't privy to the Commander's thoughts. To his sensations, to his physical reactions, and to his words – absolutely. But the majority of John's thoughts were impenetrable to Admiral Jones.

For now.

For the more Jones pushed, the more he would find. And that would be key to ultimately taking over the Commander's body.

Commander Campbell brought up a hand, locked it over his mouth, and appeared to breathe through his fingers for several seconds. "Just how much did AVA change my body? I thought she only changed my armor?"

"She altered your body sufficiently so that she could continue to communicate and help share her burden."

The Commander's eyes narrowed. "Share the burden?"

"If AVA had not altered your body and used you to help carry her consciousness, the Prime would have succumbed to her injuries far sooner. Commander Campbell, you are the only reason Leana'x is alive."

The bastard, Admiral Jones thought quickly. Not only had this fool kept Leana'x safe from Jones' assassins, but he shared the burden of AVA. Without him, Leana'x would already be dead.

Before the Admiral could give into the anger threatening to tear through his consciousness, he grabbed hold of it just in time. And he forcefully reminded himself of one fact – this was the better way. Because if the Admiral had never come here and encountered John Campbell's altered armor and mind, he would never have realized that he could possess Campbell's body and take AVA in the process.

Commander Campbell continued to breathe through his sweaty fingers before he finally allowed them to drop to his sides. He took a wary step toward the Light Guard, angling his head up toward the dark space above. "Though our ship is a pretty small light cruiser, it's going to need more room than this to land. Shouldn't we just land out on the moon?"

The Light Guard didn't answer. She simply swept her hand to the side. As soon as she did, the ground below them began to shift. It wasn't a wild, bucking move reminiscent of an earthquake. Instead it was subtle, as if the stone and dirt had all the coordination and grace of a hand gently sliding to the side.

"Whoa," Campbell managed as he shored up his position, planted his feet firmly into the ground, and darted his head quickly from left to right.

The space they were in widened. The courtyard of the palace all around simply shifted away as if it were nothing more than a mere hologram.

As soon as the ground stopped, the Light Guard took a step toward Commander Campbell. "Will this space be sufficient?"

Commander Campbell took several seconds to answer, but finally nodded his head, the move jerky. "I guess this will do. We're going to need to get out of here, though. We don't want to be burnt to a crisp by the cruiser's downward thrusters as it comes in to land."

The Light Guard simply raised a hand to the side, spreading her fingers in a sharp move. "This palace and its grounds are completely shielded. You may land your ship now," she added.

The Commander stared at her warily, and as if on cue, brought up that same hand and locked it over his mouth.

What a pathetic fool, Admiral Jones thought. A man of routine, with no ability to think on his feet. If the mere possibility that this ancient palace had sophisticated shielding like a modern Coalition heavy cruiser was enough to shake Campbell to the core, then this task would be easier than Admiral Jones had predicted.

A man who couldn't hold onto his fear in ordinary circumstances would, presumably, have a hole in his head large enough for Admiral Jones to crawl through.

Just a matter of time.

Just a goddamn matter of time, Jones kept repeating to himself like a lullaby.

For the smallest fraction of a second, he did it, even though he'd told himself there was no point. He gained full control over John's mouth muscles, and he smiled.

Quick, sharp, to the point.

It proved to the Admiral one thing – his war with Commander Campbell's consciousness would be over quickly, and there was no way the Commander would be able to win.

Chapter Eight

Commander Campbell

It took him a struggling moment to regain control of his mouth muscles. For the smallest fraction of a second, he swore they hadn't been controlled by him. As if some kind of force outside of him had reached into his mind, snapped hold of the muscles, and curled them without his permission.

He did it again, bringing up a hand, locking it on his mouth, and pressing it as hard into his lips as he could.

... He could no longer push away one fact. One gut-shaking fact. There was something wrong with him, wasn't there? That... that red light that the Admiral had used against him had changed John somehow.

But just as John became determined to turn around and ask the Light Guard for some kind of medical assistance and the use of whatever sophisticated biological scanners this palace would have, he stopped himself.

He... he just couldn't do it. He couldn't ask for help. And this wasn't just his bravado talking. This wasn't the determined Commander who just wanted to get this part of the mission done before he concentrated on his own injuries.

... John had once heard of an appalling torture technique used by the Barbarians. They had whole contingents of strong psychic warriors who'd been genetically engineered and stuffed full of implants that assisted them to use their minds to infiltrate other people's consciousnesses. It wasn't a perfect weapon. You couldn't use the psychic warriors to take over whole armies and turn them against themselves.

It was a torture technique, one used to gain intel or to just brutalize your target.

The point was... God, John couldn't shake the feeling that something like that was happening to him now. But he was far away from Barbarian lines, and the exact psychic warriors he was talking about never traveled alone. They were high-level Barbarian assets, and you wouldn't get one operating rogue.

So... what was happening to John was just stress, right?

No, wait, had he even suggested that? The word stress had just been thrown at his mind as if someone else had suggested it.

Shit. What was happening to him?

"You appear to be distracted," the Light Guard suddenly commented. She was also right in front of John. He hadn't seen her move. But that didn't mean much. He was so damn distracted right now, that a Kor assassin could jump down in front of him, sharpen its knives, do a little dance, and sing a little song, and John probably wouldn't even notice.

He still had his hand pressed against his lips, and he

just ground it there harder as if he were trying to extrude the flesh through his clenched teeth.

The Light Guard's unique eyes continued to lock on John, those little electronic cogs shifting in and out.

Maybe John should have been worried about what the Light Guard was thinking. Any ordinary person with ordinary senses would be suspicious of John right now, because he was acting damn weird. The whole goddamn galaxy was on the line, and here he was, sweating like a pig in a sauna, clamping his hand over his mouth, and withdrawing inward.

"Once this process is complete, I will take you to our medical facilities," the Light Guard said smoothly.

John dropped his hand. No, it rocketed from his mouth and pressed against his leg as he took a hard step toward her. "I'm fine. I've already told you – I'm not your priority. We have to concentrate on saving the galaxy right now. I'm standing, I'm speaking, I'm breathing, and that's good enough for me."

There was vehemence behind John's reaction. It wasn't his, either.

So where the hell did it come from?

The Light Guard didn't react. She simply pointed upward. "Deliver your ship," she said.

John swallowed. He brought up his wrist, tapping the armor two times to reveal the wrist device beneath his gauntlet. The armor moved swiftly in and out with the click of moving metal.

He tried to concentrate on his task. And it shouldn't be hard; he'd called ships in from a holding pattern in the atmosphere countless times before.

So why did he have to concentrate as if he was simultaneously walking along a wire, solving a complex algebra problem, and yet, all the while, fending himself off from an invisible attack?

The Light Guard's gaze didn't shift off him.

After at least a minute, which was way longer than it should take, John ticked his head up and nodded at her. "It's coming in now. Shouldn't we at least stand back?"

At this, she nodded, sweeping a hand to the side. He followed her until they stood under the awning of the courtyard.

Despite everything that was going on with John right now, he could appreciate how surreal this was. He'd been to technologically underdeveloped planets before, and he'd seen buildings like this. Heck, there were still some on Earth. And yet, to have the simplistic feel of the rock behind him juxtaposed with the sight of his ship sweeping in to land was one that stuck in his head. It reminded him sharply of how far the galaxy had come. All those countless races pulling themselves up by their proverbial bootstraps. Gathering the resources and knowledge of their world and using it to strike off into interstellar space. It was what the modern Coalition was built on. That kind of perseverance, adaptability, and, more than anything, the lust for exploration.

John watched as his ship came in to land.

The Light Guard hadn't been wrong. Though he could see the bright light of the cruiser's maneuvering thrusters pulse through the courtyard, by simply being under the awning, apparently that was enough not to be burnt to a crisp.

The Light Guard wasted no time. As soon as the ship had landed, even though its thrusters were still powering down, she strode forward. John could have reached out a hand to stop her, but who was he kidding? He still had absolutely no idea what this Light Guard was made of. His armor told him she was some form of hologram, but exactly what kind, it just didn't have enough data to figure out.

She was strong, solid, competent, and obviously intelligent enough to be adaptable.

If the Coalition had access to this kind of technology, it would change their ongoing shadow war with the Barbarians and the Kor, let alone the coming fight with the Force.

John took a step forward to follow the Light Guard out into the courtyard, and it happened again. As soon as he thought of the Force, he knew how he should feel. Afraid. The kind of fear a man can never feel twice in his life. This wasn't just the fear of him losing his family and friends. It wasn't even the far greater fear of losing everything he held dear in the Coalition. It was the fear of the Milky Way itself being completely destroyed, possibly all life in the universe too. It was the unique existential regret human minds weren't really made to feel on this scale.

Except he wasn't feeling it, and that was the problem.

Again, as if on their own, his lips wanted to curl. As if the thought of the Force was one he should rejoice at, not recoil from.

His head was a distracted mess of thoughts as he followed the Light Guard toward the cruiser.

He reached toward his wrist device, intending to unlock the hatch for her, but apparently she didn't need him to.

She swept a hand toward it, her fingers spreading wide, and for the first time, he noticed she had some strange markings on her fingers. He'd never seen anything like them. They were like moving tattoos of some description. And as she swept that hand toward the hatch, the tattoos lit up momentarily like little sparks of light in a darkened room.

It was enough that he heard an unmistakable clicking from inside the hatch as it obviously unlocked.

John should have balked at the fact that this woman had either the access codes or the ability to hack through Coalition technology.

He just followed her, his thoughts still centered on himself. Sorry, did he say centered? He felt like he was trapped in some kind of whirlwind, or centrifuge, maybe. Yeah, a centrifuge. One that was concentrating on pulling him apart from the inside out, separating his body from his consciousness and chucking away his mind.

That was a particularly sobering, sharp thought as he followed the Light Guard up the hatch and into the cruiser.

The Light Guard didn't say a word. She'd explicitly told John that she required him to be on the ship so that he could help her familiarize herself with Coalition technology, but obviously she was having no problem figuring out how it worked.

As she strode quickly down the corridor, her tall, statuesque, naked form stark against the clean white-grey lines around them, she spread her hands out wide. Again, John could see those little symbols on her fingers darting around, as if they were some kind of unique sense organ that was attempting to obtain as much data from the ship as it could.

If John had been fully compos mentis, maybe he would've ordered her to stop scanning the ship. Yeah, she'd already pointed out that she was technically Artaxan, and as a member of a Coalition sovereign state, she had every right to access Coalition technology. But that was a big technicality. He still didn't know enough about this woman.

"You have many thoughts," the Light Guard suddenly pointed out as she stopped halfway down the corridor and angled her head toward him. "I will advise you as I advised the Prime. Thinking appears to cause you stress, so I suggest you stop doing it."

There was about only one thing left in this entire universe that could actually center John's focus as it swept around his thoughts and body. And that was Leana'x. The mere mention of her was enough to get his heart racing in his chest. And as his heart raced, all those other confusing, treacherous sensations and thoughts were swept away like debris after a deluge.

He swallowed hard. "Just... just exactly what will happen to her if we can't get to the throne room in precisely two days?"

It wasn't something he wanted articulated. The last thing he wanted to know was every gruesome detail of how Leana'x would presumably break apart if the burden on her mind wasn't lessened by the technology in the throne room. But that was John speaking. And it was nigh time the Commander started to speak. He finally did what he should have done the second he'd arrived on this planet. He started to rely on his training. And he had such a body memory of his training – from every lesson at the Academy, to everything he'd ever been taught out on the field – that again it helped him center his attention.

"Leana'x could not control her thoughts, either. She was distressed. For you," the Light Guard said, not answering his question. "She could not be consoled. Which did further damage to her already stretched mind."

John didn't know how he should think about what the Light Guard was saying. His heart knew how to think, though. It skipped a beat, then another.

"She wanted to go out and find you. Instead, I placed her in stasis," the Light Guard answered smoothly.

"I see."

"As for your initial question. What will happen to the Prime if she cannot reach the throne room in time will be...." For the first time since John had met the Light Guard, she seemed momentarily unsure of herself. "Violent," she finally found the word she was after. "Every one of her cells will break apart. She will—"

John put a hand up quickly, the move jerky as if he was about to wrench his arm free from his shoulder. "I get it," he said in a raspy voice. "But we're going to need a backup plan. Reaching Artaxan Prime is only going to be half the problem. We still don't know what happened to the palace. Though I haven't been in contact with the Coalition for a while now, there's every possibility that the palace itself is still in lockdown. If we can't get her to the throne room—" John began, his fear getting the better of him. And it was fear that felt... more violent than it usually did. Destructive, too. As if the mere feeling was undoing him somehow.

The Light Guard's eyes were on him again, the little electronic cogs in her pupils shifting in and out. He would have given anything to figure out what she was thinking, but he doubted the sophisticated weapon would tell him. "If we face resistance within the palace, I will deal with it," the Light Guard said simply. "I have already gone over the information that is currently available on the incident with the Artaxan Royal Family," she said. "I believe I am fully capable of facing any resistance the conspiracy can throw at me."

John paused, his mouth half open, then his eyebrows ticked down hard over his eyes. "Sorry? How have you already gone over all data relating to the incident?"

"I have already completely accessed the full databases of this light cruiser. I have analyzed the information, and I am confident of my conclusion. Though it is clear that whoever is behind this conspiracy is being assisted by the Force, and it is clear the Force have given them access to sophisticated technology, they will not be ready for me," she said simply.

If it were anyone else, John would believe that this woman's words were just bravado. The arrogance of someone who'd never really been tested in battle. He had to appreciate one fact. This woman hadn't just been tested in battle. If her story was right, then she was a remnant from the Originals themselves.

That thought struck John. He took a step closer to her, his eyes widening. "How much do you know about the Force? Have you fought them?"

Though John didn't have time to appreciate this, his heart wasn't skipping in elation at the mere concept of the Force anymore. This conversation was centering him in his body in a way he couldn't comprehend.

"Yes, I have fought the Force, or at least, I have fought the foot soldiers. Even during the war, the Force only came out to fight at the very end. And it was the Originals themselves who fought the Force at that time. Myself and the other Light Guards were given the specific task of guarding the Gift and ensuring the carriers of the Gift were grown correctly."

John had a hell of a lot of things going on right now, and with his mind so overtaxed, he should probably have let that comment slide, but he couldn't. It activated that part of him that had joined the Coalition in the first place. That part of him that always sought out justice, no matter how hard it could be to find. He put up a hand. "You grew the Artaxans in order to hold AVA?" There was a hard, judgmental quality to his tone, and he wouldn't hide it for a second.

The Light Guard barely reacted. She simply tilted her

head to the side and nodded. "It was necessary. Only members of the Royal Family are changed. Other Artaxans retain their original, unaltered biology."

John's jaw hardened. "That still doesn't make it right. You didn't even let people know what you were doing. I mean, Leana'x never had any idea," he added.

"I have been separated from the Artaxan Royal Family and its current practices for millennia," the Light Guard said. "What the current practices are, I cannot tell. But I can assure you that in the past, every single Artaxan who was chosen to form part of the Royal Family line knew what they were and understood the full burden of what they would become. It was not a position that was taken lightly, and nor was it one that was given lightly," she said eloquently. Which was quite something. It was clear that this Light Guard was a seriously sophisticated creature. When John had first encountered her, her Standard Galactic Tongue had been stilted. Now it sounded as if she would be one of the greatest orators in the Senate.

"Then why did they ever leave this place?" He changed track, fully appreciating that he now had a resource he couldn't give up. This Light Guard didn't just have critical information about the Force. She understood the Artaxans and the Royal Family in a way it seemed no one else did anymore. With the almost complete destruction of the Royal Family, this knowledge could be key.

"The Queen who moved the Artaxan populace from the Expanse to their current home worlds did so on our advice," the Light Guard replied quickly.

"Why?" John's eyebrows clunked down.

"To protect this place, its technology, and its knowledge. To allow this place to be forgotten. The Force, you see, never truly left the Milky Way. Their foot soldiers remain and have always remained in some capacity. But over the centuries, that capacity has grown. It was key that the Artaxans keep the knowledge of this palace secret."

John wasn't entirely sure if he bought that excuse, but he didn't push any further. Yes, he wanted to find out everything he damn well could about not just the Artaxans, but the Force. But that had to wait, didn't it?

Saving Leana'x was his priority, he reminded himself with clenched teeth.

He didn't stop the Light Guard again as she strode confidently through the ship, quickly finding the engineering bay. It was clear that she had done exactly as she said, and she'd somehow remotely accessed and downloaded all of the information the cruiser had. She didn't need to pause and ask for directions. Nor did she need John's command codes as she accessed the locked engineering doors. She strode into the small room and quickly walked over to the panel beside the door.

She motioned toward John. "I will now attempt to upgrade this ship's propulsion systems. Please do as I say and exactly as I say."

John twitched. He didn't know why. It was a sudden muscular contraction, almost as if he'd just received a piece of news that goaded him. "Do I really need to be in this room with you?" he found himself asking. It was rude. And there was no reason for it, and yet, he still goddamn said it.

The Light Guard looked at him steadily. "This will be a delicate procedure. I'll need to supervise you. You do not know what you are doing," she added.

What she was saying was fair. It was true, too. So why did John want to snarl at her?

He stopped himself from doing that just in time, and he

nodded with the forced strength of someone used to taking orders.

The Light Guard was quick, efficient, and, just as she'd promised, didn't take her eyes off him.

John did exactly as he was told.

Problem was, he didn't really understand what he was doing.

Fortunately this light cruiser had pretty basic matter re-calibrators, and while the Light Guard got John to print out several new devices, she was the one who programmed them into the machine and installed them. In other words, John didn't have any opportunity to meddle with things.

No, wait. What? Not meddle with things as if he genuinely had a desire to stuff this up. He meant make a mistake.

... Right?

Though John was dutifully following every single dictate that the Light Guard gave him, the silence made him curl in on himself. And that was the worst possible thing that could happen. Because every single time John set his mind to trying to figure out what the hell was happening to him, he swore he felt his control over his body slipping.

He had no idea how much time passed, but eventually, the Light Guard strode toward him. "We are almost done —" she began, but she stopped abruptly as she ticked her head hard to the side.

John's eyes narrowed. "What is it? What's happening? You're not picking up some problem with Leana'x, are you?" With every word, his voice became quicker like blasts from a gun.

"I suggest you get to a communication panel," the guard said smoothly as she gestured toward one on the opposite side of the room.

John didn't immediately jump toward it, and instead locked his questioning gaze on her. "What's going on?"

"It seems the situation has become yet more complicated," the guard admitted as she once again gestured him toward the panel.

It took him a while to wrench his gaze off her as he ran toward the panel. There was no way he could walk as a new wave of fear slammed into him. Why was it that every single time it seemed like he was getting help in this situation, he'd be knocked for six again?

He just couldn't shake the feeling that whatever was waiting for him at the comms panel would be the worst hit he'd received yet.

Shaking, and with slightly sweat-slicked fingers, he accessed the communications panel, gaze darting toward the screen just above it.

Then he blanched. It was a full-bodied move, as if his circulatory system had diverted blood from his face permanently.

He also brought up a hand, curled it into a fist, and slammed it onto the console.

The move was so hard, the whole damn thing shook.

"It is not suggested that you react to this news by disassembling the ship. We will need it now more than ever."

John turned hard on his foot, his breath sharp in his chest. "This is terrible. There's no way we can take her to Artaxan Prime anymore. The second we go anywhere near the Artaxan Protectorate, we'll be shot out of the sky." John's voice was shaking. Anyone's voice would be shaking. Why?

Because this terrifying situation had twisted once more.

Someone calling themselves Prince Maqx was apparently still alive on Artaxan Prime. A member of the Royal

Family. He was 35th in line for the throne, in fact. Apparently he'd survived the assassination plot and lived to tell the tale. He'd been hiding in the palace, protecting himself from the assassins that had roved the halls looking for him for the past few weeks. Only now had he overcome them. But that wasn't the worst part. No, Prince Maqx had told the galaxy that the leader of this conspiracy had been none other than Leana'x herself. Apparently, she'd had eyes on the throne, and as the 100th, she'd needed to kill every other person in line for the throne to get there.

Prince Maqx was obviously a Replacement. But the galaxy had no way of knowing that.

And that wasn't even the worst part. According to the Coalition communications and news feeds John was accessing, the Prince had told everyone Leana'x hadn't acted alone. John had helped her.

He took another step back from the console, bringing up his hand to strike it, but before he could slam it against the expensive, breakable equipment, the Light Guard quickly stepped into his side. She didn't bother grabbing his hand this time, and instead made meaningful eye contact. "As I've already said, do not react to this news by damaging the only lifeline that we have. This ship will now be more important than ever."

It took John a few seconds to marshal his anger and lock his gaze back on her. "You don't get it. The whole galaxy is now going to be hunting us. I've checked the shielded Coalition communication lines, and it seems everyone believes this Prince Maqx's story. No one fears he's a Replacement and he's in on the conspiracy – they're trusting him."

The Light Guard simply looked at him and again shook her head to the side. "I do not believe this man's story. I have witnessed the truth. And I believe you will find that others will accept this truth if we show it to them."

John didn't know if he wanted to be gladdened or exasperated. Okay, it was nice that the extremely powerful super weapon believed him and wasn't about to hand him over to the Coalition. But at the same time, it was clear she didn't fully appreciate how much shit they were now in. Even before he'd received this message, this mission had been impossible. Now they'd need a miracle to get into the Artaxan Protectorate, let alone into the palace and the throne room.

"Though you have not read any information suggesting that the Coalition is suspicious of this story, it's dangerous to assume that your colleagues believe this," the guard said flatly. "Though I have had nothing to do with the modern galaxy, I understand one fact. To navigate space and to form a federation that governs it, the modern races of the Milky Way must believe in reason. And trust that your comrades will see it in time."

He was seriously exasperated now, and he just stared at her with a half open mouth. "Before we got to this planet, we had to bust a gut to get away from the assassins hunting Leana'x down. The conspiracy had penetrated even the furthest reaches of the Coalition. Maybe you're right. Maybe on a good day, I could just kick back and try to believe that the people of the Coalition are smart, and they'll figure out what really happened sooner rather than later. But this isn't a good day. Even before this goddamn story got out, this was already a perilous situation. We're facing a full-blown conspiracy in the Coalition. And we have no idea how large it is and how deep its roots run. If this story gets to the wrong people, and they can use their influence to spread it, then it isn't gonna matter how reasonable we spacefaring races are meant to be. The Coalition will try to stop us from getting to the Protectorate, and Leana'x will...." He choked up, incapable of putting into words what his heart just couldn't fathom.

The Light Guard's expression was completely impassive. They could've been talking about nothing more important than a complex maths problem, and not Leana'x's damn life and the future of the whole goddamn galaxy.

His expression twisted again, more anger pulsing through him. And he hadn't been lying before when he'd said that his fear now felt more destructive than it ever had before. So did his anger. Maybe his anger was worse, in fact. It was undermining him in a way that shouldn't be possible.

He went to jerk away, to run from the room, to get back to the palace, to lock eyes on Leana'x once more, just to confirm that she was still okay, but the Light Guard stepped in swiftly, obviously appreciating what he was about to do. She was so close, in fact, that he couldn't help but stare up into the rapidly shifting cogs of her electronic eyes. "Do you know the one capacity that allowed the Originals to finally push away the Force?" she asked out of the blue.

Of all the things she could have said, at least this one held John in place.

He found his brow clunking down low as he got some much-needed distance from his anger. "What are you talking about?"

"The answer, human, is hope. The Originals had what you call hope. A capacity to believe that if they tried their hardest, they had a chance of changing their future. You may believe this is a frivolous concept, and you may choose to instead think that the reason the Originals won was due to superior firepower and technology. This is a mistake. For technology is one thing, but the capacity to push past one's destructive emotions," she said, paying particular attention to the word destructive as it rolled off her tongue, "is a far more important capacity. If you control fear and you do not allow it to take and waste your mental energy, then you can set your mind to the true task of surviving."

John just stared at her. He didn't know what to say. And honestly, even if he had known what to say, he doubted he could control his lips right now.

The Light Guard continued to stare at him for several seconds until she took a sweeping step backward and arched her head toward the small pulsing drive in the middle of the engineering room. "The alterations to your propulsion system have been mostly completed. I will need to make continuous modifications while on course, but I am capable of this. Now I believe it is important that we head back to the palace."

John's heart kicked. "To check on Leana'x? It won't be long until she wakes up, right?" Again, just the mere fact of talking about Leana'x switched his mind from all of his problems. From the so-called destructive capacity of his anger and fear back to why he was here in the first place. Because he'd made a connection to the curious Leana'x, and they'd been thrown together in a fight for their lives.

"Indeed," the Light Guard answered. If the Light Guard were a person, not some strange amalgamation of holographic technology, John would almost read something into the tone she'd used. After all, she'd said indeed, not yes.

He didn't read anything into her tone. He followed her.

They left the ship, exited into the courtyard, and reached the palace. And, as if of their own accord, his hands started to form fists. One after another, pulsing in and out as if John was suddenly trying to punch something. He could feel it, too. This growing desire to hit a wall. To scream out in gut-punching aggravation.

He could try to tell himself that it was just a delayed reaction to the communication he'd received, but it felt more than that. Maybe... maybe it was the destructive capacity of anger, as the Light Guard had put it. Or maybe John Campbell couldn't begin to suspect what was really happening to him.

But he followed the Light Guard, and that was all that mattered for now.

Chapter Nine

Admiral Jones

ANGER. SO MUCH ANGER. LIKE FIRE, LIKE ACID. ALL OF it burning him. All of it forcing him to react. But he couldn't allow himself to.

Even before the Replacement Jones had left behind his body and borrowed John's, he'd had little capacity to deal with anger. It was one of the inherent problems with Replacement technology. But the fact that he had switched bodies had not changed that. Because it had always been his mind and not his form that had been broken. And now, he swore it wanted to crack all the way open like a skull that'd been hit with an ax.

Prince Maqx had acted on his own without any instruction from Jones.

The bastard. The coward, covetous bastard. Jones knew exactly what Prince Maqx wanted. He wanted to be the leader of this operation. He wanted to be the one who personally wrung Leana'x's throat. He wanted to be the man who brought back the Force to the Milky Way. So

Prince Maqx had acted. But in doing so, he'd put Admiral Jones in a perilous position. For Admiral Jones no longer had his Replacement body. He would be stuck in John Campbell's body until the day he either controlled it fully and destroyed John's mind, or his own mind was destroyed instead. But now this body was hunted. If Prince Maqx had said that only Leana'x was behind the conspiracy, that would've been bad enough, but now the Admiral had to contend with being hunted too.

He desperately wanted to strike out. He needed to destroy something, kill something. Do anything to allow the frustration and hatred building in his mind an outlet. And yet, at the same time he had to hold onto the scrap of reason he had. And that told him that if he were to dare to lose control in front of the Light Guard, it would all be over. But he couldn't help himself completely. He kept pulsing the hands of John's body in and out, not paying attention to the fear spreading through John's mind at the fact he'd lost momentary control over his limbs.

The Admiral was in such a state that he was no longer paying attention to where the Light Guard was leading him.

He just assumed they would head back to the stasis pod where Leana'x was being held.

But that was a dangerous assumption. Because the next thing the Admiral knew, they entered an unusual room. One he hadn't seen before. And one that John's armor warned was full of unknown technology.

The Admiral felt fear.

But it was too late.

...

Commander Campbell

He'd thought they were heading back to Leana'x. He needed to see her, now more than ever, because his mind kept telling him that if he could just hold her, things would start to make sense again.

"What is this place?" John asked as he took another step into the room.

The Light Guard didn't answer. She strode toward an odd looking device in the center of the room. It was a plinth of sorts, and on the top of it was a small red orb. As she approached, it began to glow, brighter and brighter until she set her fingers on top of it, and it reacted with a chirp.

She turned sharply on her foot and swept her hand to the side, the ball immediately flying from her grip and sailing toward John.

He tried to jerk back, but the orb was faster.

It attached to the center of his armor with a crunch like bone on bone.

"What the hell is this?" he asked, his vehemence not his own. It came from the same place that unruly anger was springing from. And it was enough to force him forward quickly.

But he could only take a step until his armor did something. It straightened. His arms snapped beside him, his legs stiffened, and he stood as if to attention.

He could just move his mouth, and that was all it took to snap his stiff lips open. "What the hell are you doing?" he demanded once more.

The Light Guard simply looked at him. Then she inclined her head all the way to the side. The move would have been natural, were it not for the fact she was extending her neck way beyond the ordinary capacity of an Artaxan. "It is necessary," she said. And without further explanation, she turned hard on her foot and walked out of there.

She left him alone. There was nothing he could do to move, let alone hope to follow her. His armor had been locked down completely.

A second later, he could feel something initiate his helmet, and it snapped in place over his head with a hiss.

"Hey, come back! Come back!" he screamed. The little red orb that had landed on his chest continued to pulse. In and out, in and out, almost like a heart that was trying to remind his how to beat.

But John's heart didn't need any reminders, and as it kept pounding away in his chest, he felt something slip from him.

It was his control.

Chapter Ten

Leana'x

She woke slowly. Her mind just didn't want to be roused.

It took a while to remember where she was. Slowly, her eyes started to adjust to the semi-darkness, and she was aware of the closed pod hatch in front of her.

She could just see someone peering at her in front of the glass.

Her heart suddenly leaped into her chest.

"John—" she began, but she stopped as the pod hatch released. With a cloud of atmosphere discharging in every direction, she saw the open pod reveal Na'van.

"You have awoken. Though that pod has lightened some of the load on your body and kick started the healing process, there is only so much it can do. We must take you to the ship at once and transport you to Artaxan Prime," Na'van said without any explanation.

Leana'x only listened with half an ear as she leaned out of the pod.

... She... for some reasons she'd thought John would be here. She... she could almost remember him staring at her through the pod hatch.

"I... John was here... he," she began. But then she stopped abruptly as she realized the last time she'd actually seen John, he'd been outside battling with the Admiral.

Na'van took a step in and immediately reached a hand through the pod and locked her hand against Leana'x's shoulder. "Do not become emotional. Strong emotions will wear your body down even further. We are now in a race against time to get you to the throne room before your mind and body fully degrade."

Leana'x couldn't blink back her shock, even though she tried, her eyelids looking like frantic camera shutters. "What are you talking about? Wait, it doesn't matter – tell me where John is. Did you manage to save him from the Admiral?"

At first it seemed as if Na'van wouldn't answer. And there was an... odd expression on the hologram's face as she considered Leana'x quietly. "He was saved," she finally revealed.

Leana'x's heart could have fallen from her chest right into her hands. She took such a massive sigh, it practically propelled her out of the pod.

Na'van didn't move her hand. "As I said before, please refrain from having any strong emotions. Also, do not move quickly or overtax yourself in any way."

Leana'x couldn't listen. "I need to see John," she managed as she pushed out of the pod.

She went to place a foot on the floor, but her knee gave way, her legs like string.

Before she could fall and strike her head on the hard side of the pod, Na'van stepped in swiftly and looped an arm around Leana'x's legs, holding her aloft in a quick, practiced move. "You cannot stand. The non-essential processes of your body have been all but shut down to redistribute power toward essential systems."

There was a lot Leana'x could have pointed out at that statement. For one, the way Na'van was describing Leana'x's body was like a set of mechanical structures. Her legs and the ability to stand, let alone run, were hardly non-essential systems.

But Leana'x only cared about one thing right now. "Please take me to see John. Is he alright? Has he been hurt? Is he conscious? Why isn't he here?" she couldn't cram her questions out fast enough.

Na'van looked down at her, the hologram's electronic eyes focusing on Leana'x in full. "He is being held in body lock until the palace's scanners can determine what's wrong with him," Na'van revealed without any further explanation.

Leana'x froze. "Wait... what? What does that mean? Is he injured?"

"Injured?" Na'van looked to the side, her expression one of controlled confusion. "I do not know. However, he has been altered. I initially assumed his fight with the Replacement Admiral Jones left him with no permanent damage. I was wrong."

Leana'x started shaking her head, her face banging up against Na'van's arm. "What do you mean? Please tell me he'll be alright."

"I cannot tell you that he'll be alright. Only time will tell." With that, Na'van walked forward toward the door. It reacted as she approached, sweeping to the side to reveal a new stone corridor beyond.

It was now clear that the palace walls, doors, and rooms

were alive somehow. And if not alive, then fully capable of seamless movement. Leana'x hadn't heard the shifting of gears or stone, and yet a new corridor was now waiting outside.

Na'van strode down it quickly. She didn't seem taxed by the fact she was carrying Leana'x, and could probably have hefted ten men without trouble. Or maybe more – after all, Leana'x had no idea what the full range of this hologram's abilities were.

Though Leana'x was bursting with questions, she didn't have the time to ask them. Na'van took several swift steps down the corridor, only for a door to appear by her side. She smoothly pivoted on her foot and strode in.

Leana'x screamed.

It was John. Right there. Just a few meters in front of her.

He was strung up in the air like a man to a cross. His arms were spread to his sides, his legs limp, and his head on an angle as it rested against his chest. There was a pulsing red orb on his armor, probably the source of the field locking him in place.

His helmet was on, but she still knew it was him as she reached a shaking hand forward. "What's happening to him? What's going on? Why is he suspended like that?"

"He is being scanned. His body and armor have also been suspended until the results of the scan can be determined."

"What are you talking about? What exactly are you looking for?" Leana'x was becoming more exasperated with every second as she stared at John's limp, strung-up form.

It was a fact Na'van noticed as she tilted her head down. "As I have already told you, please do not become emotionally affected."

"If you want me to be calm, then let him the hell down and tell me what's going on!"

Na'van paused as she appeared to appreciate that Leana'x didn't have some handy emotion switch in her head she could just flick. And nor was she ever going to let this drop, despite the fact it was apparently doing her damage.

The hologram actually sighed, as if she were capable of frustration. "John Campbell's mind and body have been altered by a form of Replacement technology. Why, I cannot tell. I have gathered sufficient information from observing him to conclude that he is not in full control of his body. At least, not all of the time."

Leana'x felt like Na'van was slapping her, over and over again with each word. It took so long for Leana'x to be able to open her lips a crack, and hiss, "What?" Not... not in control of his own body?"

"Though I have never seen Replacement technology used in this way, and did not for that reason originally discern what had happened to the Commander, I believe I understand what transpired now."

"What do you mean?"

"During the Commander's fight with the Admiral, the Admiral locked the Commander in some kind of radiation field. At first, I assumed the radiation was benign. It wasn't. During the fight, the Admiral also died. At first, I assumed his Replacement body failed. It didn't."

"Just... please tell me what's happening to John."

"It is my belief that the Replacement Admiral Jones' mind is now sharing the Commander's body. And by sharing, I mean attempting to take over."

Leana'x reeled. She felt cold all over – truly, crushingly cold. The kind of cold that went light years beyond being stuck in a freezer. This was the cold that could only be associated with being stuck in the wastes of deep space, way beyond life and way beyond even the slimmest possibility of rescue.

And, importantly, this was the kind of cold that Leana'x's already taxed body simply couldn't afford to feel right now.

Na'van suddenly jerked her head down. "Be calm. I am explaining everything to you. Do not lose hope, either. I have no intention of letting the Commander's body be taken over by the Replacement Admiral Jones. That is why the Commander is now in lockdown as I search for a way to remove Admiral Jones."

The cold started to thaw.

Leana'x didn't know what to think. She didn't know what to say. She knew what she wanted to do, though. Wrench herself free from Na'van's arms and run toward John's limp body. But there was no way Na'van was going to let her go, and even if she did, Leana'x doubted she could move right now. So she just lay there in Na'van's arms, staring at John.

She could barely process what she'd just been told.

How... how could John's mind have been taken over by the Admiral?

"As I have already told you multiple times before, you should resist—" Na'van began.

Leana'x forced herself to swallow, and she ground her eyes tightly closed. "I get it. I get it. I need to calm down. But how the hell am I meant to calm down when he's... he's being taken over?"

"Do not become unduly distressed. I'm assessing the situation. And I will be able to come up with a solution."

Leana'x snapped her head hard to the side, almost doing herself an injury as she stared desperately at Na'van. "You mean there's definitely a way to save him?" Her voice was so damn breathy, it sounded like she was being choked.

Na'van momentarily looked as if she regretted her words, and it took her a while to make eye contact. "There may be a way to save him," she said, her tone qualified and careful.

It happened again. Leana'x felt as if her entire world was falling out from underneath her. How... how could this kind of stuff keep happening to her? From being almost assassinated several times on the *Hercules*, to only just making it into the palace. Now this?

Leana'x felt like she was the most cursed person in the world.

She felt Na'van's eyes on her. "As Prime, you must be stronger than this," Na'van said flatly.

Out of all of the things that Na'van could've said, that one got Leana'x's attention, because it appealed to something Leana'x hadn't yet had the chance to grapple with.

Beyond all the adventure and all of her fraught attempts at survival, she was the Prime. And the only way that was going to change was if she died.

And if she died? Oh heck, the rest of the Artaxan Protectorate and quite possibly the Coalition would go with her.

Na'van didn't blink once, and Leana'x doubted the hologram needed to. But that meant the view of the Light Guard's electronic eyes was never dulled, if even for a second. "A Prime must carry the burden of the Gift. Not just for herself, but the galaxy as a whole. Not just for the Artaxans, but for everyone," Na'van's voice changed, becoming louder, becoming graver, as if she were some god proclaiming the one and only truth.

Leana'x wanted to look away. She wanted to recede into

herself, but she forced herself to face Na'van. "I didn't ask to be the Prime," Leana'x said before she could stop herself. From the stress to the fear to the fact her body felt as if it had been shoved into an engine core assembly, she just couldn't deal with this anymore. She didn't want to. She wanted to go back to the simple days aboard the *Hercules*, even if it meant John reverting to the arrogant bastard he'd been. She'd give anything – anything to free him from Admiral Jones' clutches.

At first, Na'van didn't react. She never, ever stopped staring. But she certainly didn't reach up, slap Leana'x, and tell her to get a handle on herself for the rest of the galaxy.

In fact, Leana'x was the first to react as she deliberately hardened her jaw, lowered her gaze, and allowed it to slice back toward John. "This isn't fair," she said.

"It was never designed to be fair. Though I appreciate that the modern traditions of the Artaxan Royal Family have changed, and you are no longer taught the true knowledge, I would like to believe that no one in your training ever told you this would be fair."

Leana'x took a moment, but then she nodded. Na'van was right. The Artaxan Royal Family was a lot of things. But not once in her training had someone ever said that being a member of the Royal Family came down to luck. No, they'd used the words privilege and responsibility. As a member of the Royal Family and to be in line for the Prime throne was to serve your people in a way few others ever could. And it was a service that would take you, body, mind, and soul.

Leana'x was only now appreciating what that meant as she brought a hand up, flattened it on her head, and tried desperately to calm her thoughts and the pain ripping through her temples.

"You may not have asked to be Prime, but now you are Prime. And there are no others. If you fail in your role of holding the Gift, the Force will come," Na'van said blankly.

It was like a slap in the face. Bemoaning what had happened to Leana'x was one thing, torturing herself over the fact she'd dragged John into this was another. But being told that if she was weak – even for a second – she'd be responsible for the Force destroying the universe, that was as bad as it sounded.

She forced a breath, then another. She ensured her neck was held out as high as she could make it, even though she was still cradled in Na'van's arms. She lifted her chin, too. In other words, she went through all the motions. She tried to look like the queen everyone was telling her she was.

Then she settled her gaze back on John. "So there's something you can do for him?" she asked, for the first time since she'd seen him, her tone remaining almost neutral.

"We shall see. But first, we must transport you to Artaxan Prime. You must go to the throne room before it's too late. Commander John Campbell can wait here until we return."

"*No,*" Leana'x screamed. It was unhinged, it was loud, and her voice echoed through the room, punching out like a clap of thunder.

It also wasn't her own.

For a split second, it looked as if Na'van wanted to react again, no doubt taking the opportunity to tell Leana'x once more that as the last Prime, she could no longer be selfish. But Na'van stopped. The hologram's eyes narrowly focused on Leana'x. The Light Guard's pupils changed, momentarily glowing a different color, almost as if she was scanning Leana'x on some different spectrum.

Leana'x could feel it too. Though most of the vehemence had been her own, some of it had come from something else. And that other place was AVA.

Leana'x hadn't connected with AVA for a long time, and either the stasis pod had helped heal the connection, or the very thought of leaving John behind was enough to force AVA to resurface, despite the damage it could do to her.

The Light Guard didn't push. No more arguments. It was clear who her master truly was. Na'van nodded her head low. "Very well. We will not leave him. We will take him. You have my word," she added, voice grating down low as she again bowed.

Leana'x let out a relieved breath. Then, almost immediately, she was hit in the center of her head with what felt like a battering ram. It honestly seemed like somebody had shoved a skewer up her nose and started to scramble her brains about.

She groaned, jolted her head back, and covered her face with both her hands.

Then she felt a wet slick of blood over her palms.

She heard the Light Guard hiss. "You have my word," she said once more. "We will bring him. Despite the fact it is... unwise," Na'van added.

It took Leana'x a seriously long time to be able to pull her hands down, to wipe the blood from her nose, to settle her gaze back on John. She was panting as if she'd just run a mile, even though she'd been cradled the entire time.

... Which meant she was really injured, didn't it? Despite what that stasis pod had done for her, Leana'x was still on death's door.

She felt this dense kind of pressure settle through her heart and spread, feeling like it was trying to take over her body and possess her like a ghost.

And that ghost was the knowledge that even if she tried

her hardest, there was a real possibility Leana'x wouldn't see this through.

She was just too damaged.

"My advice to you is to now withdraw in as much as you can. Utilize meditation techniques taught to you by the Artaxan Royal Family. Concentrate only on keeping yourself safe. Allow the rest of this mission to be undertaken by me. You have my word that I will do everything I can to keep you safe."

"And—" Leana'x began automatically.

"Commander Campbell too. I have no intention of letting him die. Though it would have been... best for your personal security to leave him here until I establish you in the throne room, I now appreciate he must come."

Leana'x let out another relieved breath. Her eyes partially closed, too. But then she forced them open. She stared at John. "I want to talk to him," she said. "Can I talk to him? Or is that... impediment field holding him in some kind of stasis?"

The Light Guard appeared to think. Leana'x could see it as Na'van focused her gaze on John, and the hologram's expression became blank.

Just when Leana'x thought that Na'van wouldn't comply, she brought up a hand, easily cradling Leana'x with just one arm, and Na'van spread her fingers to the side.

John's helmet receded, showing his head.

And for the first time since Leana'x had walked into the room, he finally pulled his head up, his body no longer completely limp.

She watched as his eyes dilated, as his gaze focused on her. Then the relief – the heart-shaking relief that spread across his features, lit up his cheeks, and sent a powerful emotion almost like love blazing through his eyes.

"Leana'x. Leana'x! You're alright. You're alive. Thank God."

"John," she said as she tried to bring up a hand and reach toward him.

Na'van immediately grabbed her hand and gently pulled it down. "Do not tax yourself," she said.

Though John appeared to want to stare at Leana'x forevermore, his gaze quickly sliced toward Na'van. It seemed to take him a minute, then his brow crumpled with suspicion. "What have you done to me? Let me go. Whatever you're planning—"

"I have already explained this to you, but I will explain again. Commander John Campbell, you have been altered. Your consciousness is currently being possessed by the Replacement mind of Admiral James Jones. You are no longer yourself," Na'van said with some finality.

John's mouth opened. There was a real hard click to his jaw, almost as if he was getting ready to wrench it off and throw it right at Na'van. His eyes momentarily blazed with anger, too.

Then, almost like a fire going out, that violent anger was completely subsumed.

She watched fear crumple John's features.

It made Leana'x want to reach out a hand to him, but Na'van was still holding Leana'x's hand down.

"I do not advise you to become too emotionally passionate until I understand more about this process," Na'van explained to John.

"... I... don't... believe..." he trailed off.

The look in John's eyes was a crippling one. Leana'x had never seen anything so powerful. It was like looking at somebody as they realized their entire life was about to crumble. Everything they knew, everything they held dear, everything they thought about themselves – it was about to become completely irrelevant. It was about to be crushed by some vicious force, and there wasn't a goddamn thing they could do.

Tears started to trail down Leana'x's cheeks, and she let out the smallest sob.

That saw was enough to pull John out of himself for a few seconds. He offered her a sad smile. "Leana'x, it's okay," he said as he forced himself to clench his teeth. Then he leveled his gaze at Na'van once more. "I think you can trust that hologram," he said. "Or at least I hope you can trust her. Because if you can't – if this is some kind of game. If you're here to hurt Leana'x—"

Na'van immediately brought up a hand. She spread her fingers wide in a placating move. But it was a forceful one. "As I have already reminded you several times, Commander Campbell, do not become emotionally passionate. I believe strong, destructive emotions, such as fear and anger, will allow the Replacement mind of Admiral Jones to take further root. You must attempt to control yourself." Though Na'van's tone was usually flat, now, it was hard.

Leana'x watched John blink. There was an... erratic quality to it. Though his left eye blinked fine, his right twitched a little.

She suddenly curled her hand into a tight fist as she swore she saw it, just for a second. Just for a flicker.

Something vicious looking back at her. Something violent. Something that wanted to pick John's hands up, wrap them around Leana'x's throat, and squeeze until she took her last breath.

Up until that moment, Leana'x hadn't really believed what Na'van had said.

Now she receded back into Na'van's arms.

Out of the corner of her eye, Leana'x could tell that Na'van's gaze narrowed. "Control yourself," she said with a stiff tone. "It is now up to you, Commander Campbell. Though it would be preferable to leave you here in stasis until I can understand more of this process and attempt to save what remains of your consciousness, that is no longer an option. I must take you aboard your cruiser, and it lacks the technical facilities that are in this palace. You will be placed in the brig, and though I will attempt to assist you, the fight between you and the Replacement Admiral James Jones' mind will be down to you," she said with finality.

John's eyes stopped twitching. Every last flicker of anger disappeared, and he swallowed hard, his throat pressing against the unyielding collar of his armor.

He didn't say a word.

He didn't have to.

Leana'x had led a relatively privileged life. She'd led a relatively quiet and peaceful one, too. Though she'd been involved in a few skirmishes at the Academy and in training, she wasn't prepared for anything like this. This was the kind of situation they talked about in the Academy but very few people would ever face. Because it was the kind of situation that would only ever come up once in several hundred years. The fate of the goddamn galaxy now rested in her hands. More than that, it rested in John's. But his hands were no longer completely his own. A fact that was evidenced as his hands suddenly clutched into the tightest, most bloodless fists.

Instantly, Na'van's eyes locked on them, and she slowly ticked her gaze up to face John. "Control yourself. Your fate is now literally in your hands."

There was a moment, a moment where Leana'x feared

the worst as a sudden muscular twitch passed over John's face and darted hard into his brow.

Leana'x was aware of her heart as it beat frantically in her chest, aware of her fear as it climbed around the base of her spine.

But then John relaxed. It was hard to tell, as she couldn't see the micro movements of his muscles, shoulders, and legs, as they were still obscured by the bulk of his armor. But she could see his face. And as she gazed into his eyes, she saw it once more – that somber sorrow. The fear of the situation, and, more than anything, his aching sadness at what was happening to her.

He half closed his eyes. "I understand. I'll do what I can. But... don't... don't leave me alone with Leana'x," he said.

A thrill of fear raced hard through Leana'x's back, snapped into her jaw, pulsed into her heart, and felt like it would tear her to shreds.

Na'van wrenched her gaze off John and locked it on Leana'x. "For your own good, Prime, you must now leave this room."

"No. Wait. Please, John—"

She looked up at John, and he looked down at her. She didn't think she'd ever seen somebody look as truly sad as John.

There was a gut-aching quality to it, one that made her heart want to reach out to him.

"It's okay, Leana'x," he said in a quiet voice that could barely carry. "This is for the best. Now go. Concentrate on keeping yourself safe. I'll... I'll fight him off," he said, voice choked.

Tears started to stream down Leana'x's cheeks. Though she'd decided several moments before to start acting like a

Prime, that decision didn't count right now. Nothing but her grief did.

Without another word, Na'van turned on her foot and walked out of the room.

Leana'x tried to crane her head over Na'van's shoulder, but with two swift steps, the hologram was out of the room.

The door closed behind them, and once more, they were in one of the cold stone corridors of the palace.

Tears started to freely streak down Leana'x's cheeks now, and she made no attempt to stop herself from sobbing.

Na'van didn't pause and strode quickly down the corridor.

When Leana'x stopped paying attention to her grief for half a second, she could appreciate that the palace was changing around them. She could pick up the subtlest feel of shifting, grating stone.

And, again, if she truly concentrated, she swore she could pick up that... intelligence. It seemed to be imbued in the very building. As if it were alive.

If she were in any other condition, she'd ask about it. Give in to her curiosity. A building that shifted all of its own accord and had its own sentience was something a dutiful explorer should investigate.

But Leana'x didn't care. Couldn't care.

She just lay there meekly in Na'van's arms as the Light Guard strode through the halls of the palace and out into a courtyard.

The cruiser Leana'x and John had taken from the *Hercules* was sitting in the courtyard. It was glistening under a midmorning sun, the sunlight slicing off the smooth white-gray hull. It also lit up the unmistakable Coalition emblem that was emblazoned over both sides of the hull.

For a split second, Leana'x forced herself to pay attention to that emblem. She let her eyes track along it.

She let it remind her of why she joined the Coalition in the first place. It wasn't just to get away from her people, from her position as the hundredth.

It was to explore the galaxy, right?

To make a difference?

To make a difference, she whispered in her head.

And this was making a difference. Even if it was the hardest damn thing she would ever do.

"You are calming. I suggest whatever you are doing, you concentrate on it. Are you utilizing the specific meditation techniques the Artaxan Royal Family were taught?" Na'van asked.

Leana'x took a moment to answer. "Kind of," she lied.

Or did she lie?

Because the one rule to meditation was focus. Maybe she wasn't currently focusing on the flickering light of a candle, but she was focusing on something far more important. The principle she lived her life by and yet one she'd never really assessed.

Just why had she left Artaxan Prime?

Why had she left the Royal Family behind?

Was it just to be free of their arrogance? Was it just to be treated like a normal person?

Or had it been because she wanted to strike out and make her own story?

Well she was certainly making her own story now. Her own history, too.

Na'van wasted no more time in approaching the ship. Leana'x swore she could feel something – this... sudden mental interference. No, not interference – almost like a radio picking up a message from another line.

A second later, as Na'van approached the back of the cruiser, the hatch door opened of its own accord and a ramp built itself, stopping just a centimeter in front of Na'van's feet.

... So Na'van was capable of mental communication with technology, ha? It made sense. Even if Na'van would never have seen a Coalition ship before, considering she'd been trapped in this palace for countless millennia.

But that wasn't even the point. The point was, whatever type of communication Na'van had just used, Leana'x had kind of felt it, hadn't she?

"What exactly are you?" Leana'x asked, giving in to her curiosity. "You're not a hologram, are you? You're made of light, but more, right? And it's not some accident that you mostly resemble an Artaxan, right?"

Na'van cut her gaze down toward Leana'x as she walked in through the hatch of the ship. "I am a form of technology that no longer exists and one you do not have the grounding to understand," she answered opaquely.

"But you're like me, aren't you? You've... been genetically altered somehow. You're not just light," Leana'x said, making things up on the fly.

She was sure of what she felt, though. That form of mental communication had been familiar.

Na'van arched an eyebrow. "You are correct. I am not just light. I am what occurs at the intersection of light and life," she said. And if her previous statements had been opaque, it was nothing compared to this doozy.

She was what occurred at the intersection of light and life? Light, by its very nature, could not form biological entities. It couldn't form structures with bonds, let alone with enough temporal and spatial consistency to allow for consciousness.

Or at least, that was what you were taught in the Coalition.

Na'van continued to stare down at Leana'x. "The Originals were capable of an understanding that no other group of races have achieved since their death."

"Capable of understanding? What does that mean?"

Na'van ticked her head back. It was clear the conversation was over. "I will now place you in the bridge. I will lock the door and secure you in there until I have transferred the Commander to the brig. I will leave you with full control of the bridge's defensive capacities. I will also leave you with a weapon to defend yourself. Though I do not believe there are any other assassins on this moon, I now appreciate that we must be careful."

Leana'x blinked hard, realizing she now had to pay attention more than ever.

With Na'van's long legs, they reached the bridge swiftly. Again the hologram didn't pause, and she ticked her head toward the bridge, mentally activating the door. With a swish, it opened.

She walked in.

Na'van placed Leana'x down carefully in the command chair.

Leana'x's body still felt so weak, she knew she couldn't stand, let alone hope to run.

Na'van leaned over and flattened a hand on the control panel directly behind Leana'x.

Leana'x arched her head over her shoulder to see what Na'van was doing, and it was just in time to see a stream of data suddenly spring across the view screen as it flickered into life.

The data moved so quickly that Leana'x had absolutely no hope of figuring out what it meant.

There was a beep. "Defensive capacities upgraded. Command control now shared between the entity called Na'van and Ensign Leana'x."

Na'van blinked twice, and as she did, her eyes changed. Not just the color, the structure of the cogs within them.

A thrill of something chased hard up Leana'x's back, and again she felt Na'van communicating mentally with the ship.

But though Leana'x was aware of what was happening, she couldn't intercept the messages, let alone hope to figure out what Na'van was doing.

Na'van abruptly took a step back and nodded at Leana'x. Then she reached around her back and grabbed a gun. Except the only problem was, the gun hadn't been holstered behind the naked hologram's back a second before. And yet, as Na'van reached a hand around and spread it behind her back, something formed there with a spark of light.

Leana'x blinked quickly as Na'van reached around and placed the gun in Leana'x's lap.

"Point and shoot," Na'van commanded simply.

"I... I've never seen a firearm like this. What kind of destructive capacity does it have?"

Na'van paused. "Practically endless."

Leana'x opened her eyes wide, her eyebrows peaking toward her hairline. "I'm sorry? Practically endless? That isn't a real measure—"

"All you need to do is point and shoot. This firearm is sufficiently sophisticated to adjust its setting to destroy whatever is in front of you, unless such a thing possesses high-level Force armor. But as I have not seen such armor since the days of the Original War, it is unlikely that you will be assailed by it. Now – prepare to defend yourself. But as I have said, it is very unlikely anyone is out there." Na'van took a step back.

Leana'x kind of wanted to reach a hand out to her. She didn't entirely know why, either. Was it to hold the hologram in place so Leana'x could figure out more about this apparently infinitely destructive weapon? Was it to find out more about the unique form of mental communication Na'van had with the computer?

Or was it just because Na'van was pretty much Leana'x's only hope of survival now?

Leana'x's training and better judgment won out, and she let her hand fall into her lap. She nodded, carefully placing her hands around the gun. "I've got it. I can look after myself. Go get John," she said, voice cracking on the word John.

Na'van wasted no more time, turned swiftly on her foot, and strode out of the bridge.

As soon as the hologram was past the door, the bridge door closed with a snap. There was a unique buzz, too, and a second later, a force field stronger than Leana'x had ever seen flickered over the door. She blinked hard as she watched that same force field form around the room, marching up the consoles, even covering the view screen.

She jerked back in her chair, and it floated back until it was in the center of the room.

She stared at the force field, then ticked her gaze toward the view screen.

It was blank. Though Leana'x could have told it to show the view of what was happening outside, she closed her eyes instead.

She kept her fingers clutched around the gun, and Leana'x, the new Prime of the Artaxan Protectorate, tried to keep calm.

Chapter Eleven

Admiral Jones

The bastards. All of them. Fools. Greedy. Livestock that didn't know when to die.

He was going out of his mind. Which was saying something, as he was no longer technically in his mind.

But the rage was bellowing through him now. It was ripping, tearing, getting ready to destroy everything in its path.

Because there was no point in controlling himself anymore.

The idiot John Campbell knew.

And the idiot John Campbell was trying to fight back.

The Replacement James Jones had no real way of explaining what it was like to be trapped in someone else's mind while they actively tried to push him away. Ordinary spatial language just didn't cut it. He couldn't begin to explain the strange sensations of being amorphous and without a body, and yet connected enough to still recognize he was a single consciousness. One that was being assailed from every side.

But even though the fool John Campbell was pulling out every stop and using every pathetic scrap of his training and determination to try to push Jones back, there was no way the Admiral was going to give up.

This would be a fight down to the death, and the Replacement James Jones would not be the one to die.

Instead, he kept waiting. Bolstering his defenses as he did, bolstering his anger, too. Letting it pump into him as if his consciousness was now a reservoir purely for hatred. For the more hatred he could collect, the more powerful he would become when he turned that hatred against John Campbell.

The opportunity would come.

The opportunity would come.

And when it did, the Replacement James Jones would take it with both hands.

...

Commander Campbell

He... couldn't describe this.

Would anyone be able to describe this?

He was trapped in his own mind. And for God's sake, there was a monster trapped in his mind with him. His body, too.

John didn't think he'd ever been paler. There'd never been a reason to be as pale as this. Even when he'd lost his parents on the colony, even when Leana'x had been attacked those three times on the *Hercules*, it hadn't felt like this.

Because back then, John had had his body. And with his

body, he'd been able to make a difference. With his desperation and determination, he'd been able to fight.

But right now, his body wasn't completely his own.

John couldn't even begin to describe the torture his mind was going through as he remained there frozen on the spot, suspended in the air, his armor locked down with no hope of ever being able to move again.

But before he could wallow in his self-pity for too long, the doors in front of him opened, and the Light Guard walked back in.

She had a truly striking form. And though she was technically naked, that didn't reduce her power at all. It almost magnified it.

She looked as if she was some kind of fundamental form, if that made any sense. Some amalgam of the most powerful qualities of the alien races of old.

She strode right up to John, stopped with her hands rested by her sides, tilted her head up, and locked her unique electronic eyes on him. "To win the war against the Admiral, you must be stronger. To be stronger, you must never give in to destructive emotions. You must force your way past them, finding an alternative route. Do you understand?"

No. To be honest, John didn't understand. What she was saying was just words, a collection of breaths, just syllables, just sounds. She couldn't begin to understand what was happening in his mind, because he couldn't understand it, either. There was no lexicon in any Galactic tongue that could help him comprehend what was happening inside his own goddamn head.

He hardened his jaw.

She narrowed her eyes.

"We do not have time. I must now remove you from the

impediment field. Once I do, the fight will begin in full. Do you understand?" she questioned once more.

He opened his mouth, the movements of his lips vicious, as if they were whips he was trying to crack through the air. But just before he could snap at her, he stopped, and he forced himself to let her words actually settle in.

... The impediment field was meant to be helping him somehow? And when it was turned off, this war in his head would only get worse?

Dear God.

He knew he paled even more. So her eyes narrowed even further. "I want to give you more time to learn how to defend yourself, but I can't," she said, and without further pause, she brought her hand up and ticked it to the side.

The impediment field holding John in place stopped. It snapped like a bough that had just been wrenched from a tree. The red pulsing ball that had produced it flew from his chest and settled back on top of its plinth.

The Light Guard made no attempt whatsoever to catch John as he fell. He crumpled on the ground, his armor striking the resonant floor with a thump that echoed through the room.

His body didn't jolt, and God knows he didn't break anything.

Or wait... maybe something did break.

Because in a rush, he felt Admiral James Jones. In full.

John couldn't comprehend how the Admiral had been hiding in his head for so long without giving away his presence. But now it felt like there was a balloon right in the center of John's brain – one that was getting bigger by the second, one that just wanted to cram the rest of his consciousness out.

He screamed as he brought up a hand, latched it on his

head, and started to press his gauntlet-covered fingers harder and harder into his brow until he started to draw blood.

The Light Guard snapped forward, grabbed his hands, wrenched them to the side, despite his sophisticated armor, and promptly threw him over her shoulder.

It happened in such a flash, that even if John hadn't been dealing with a psychopath in his head, there would've been nothing he would've been able to do to stop her.

He was suddenly distracted by the question of just how powerful this woman was. That distraction couldn't last.

Though he couldn't hear Admiral Jones, he could feel the man, punching and kicking, trying to tear down John's defenses.

"Concentrate, and fight," the Light Guard snapped as she whirled hard on her foot and strode toward the door. She didn't need to make a motion, it opened at her approach. She turned hard on her foot, stalked down the corridor, and headed through the palace.

Though there would've once been a time that John would have been intrigued by the ancient building around him, he couldn't even appreciate where he was anymore. He got the distinct desire to begin to hit his head against the Light Guard's back in place of trying to wrench his brain free with his hands.

But then the Light Guard simply snapped, "Control yourself," once more. Her voice was low, a warning note echoing out as loud as a blast from a horn.

Control himself.

Shit, control himself. Did she know what she was asking? Did she know what was happening inside his head?

John wasn't trained for this. Yeah, okay, so he'd undergone the same psychic defense classes that most other high-level operatives had at the Academy. And, yeah, he'd been learning how to communicate with Leana'x, too. But this... it was on a completely different level.

He just couldn't....

Before John knew what was happening, they reached the courtyard, and the Light Guard swiftly took him in through the open hatch of the cruiser and into the ship.

The hatch receded without a single command from the Light Guard – or at least, a verbal one.

With a shudder, the hatch sealed shut, and he heard the unmistakable hiss of atmosphere reinstating.

Na'van strode through the back of the ship until she reached the brig.

She approached the door, it opened, and again, without a single command, he heard the unmistakable click of the security field begin to initiate.

By the time she strode into the brig, the cell on the opposite side of the room was starting to prep. A heavy hum filled the air, and even from here, John's armor could pick up the electrical load getting ready to snap in place and initiate the level X force field that would block the cell from the rest of the ship.

Na'van strode right into the cell just as the force field was forming. Though at first John's stomach pitched as he realized that both of them would be torn apart, Na'van obviously possessed some serious defenses, because she was completely unharmed as the force field formed in front of her. So was John.

She strode in and practically dumped him on the small hard metal bench that ran along the opposite wall – the only furniture in the cell, if you could call it that.

He sat with a thump, his arms and legs loose, his head momentarily flopping down onto his chest. It took several seconds for him to regain enough control to lift his face up. It was in time to see Na'van take several steps back. She walked backward through the force field, the massive electrical load discharging and crackling around her form, but not affecting it for a second.

She stopped outside the force field and stared at him, her electronic eyes focusing in and out. "I will keep my eyes on you," she said.

By eyes, he was pretty sure she meant her full sensor capacity.

His body was still limp, his arms loose between his knees, his head just held aloft. His expression, however, was hard. At least, one side of his face was. He momentarily lost control of it, and he could feel a sneer flick over the left side of his lips.

He still had control of his right side, and he blinked, opening his mouth as wide as he could. "I need you... I need you to promise me something," he said.

The Light Guard ticked her head to the side, her eyes narrowing. "I cannot promise to save you. I can only promise to try," she said.

He shook his head. It was a truly jerky move, because he only had control over one side of his body. "That's not it. I need... I need you to promise to end me... to kill me if things get out of hand. Do you... understand?"

Na'van locked her eyes on him. "You do not need to ask. It will happen," she said blankly. "Though I know I must attempt to protect you because you too help to carry the burden of AVA, at the same time, I cannot allow the Prime to die. If the situation dictates, you attempt to kill her, and there is no way to save you—"

"Then you kill me," John said with a massive sigh as he finally regained control of his body and sat straight. He nodded. "Good," he said, voice hoarse but words strong. "Good. That's all I need to know."

Na'van stared at him for several seconds. "I cannot offer you any advice other than this— if you were an ordinary human, the Replacement would not have been able to possess you. Whatever changes AVA made to your mind have allowed Admiral Jones in. But know this," she added before John's stomach could sink at the prospect that this was all down to AVA, "those changes can also help you. I suggest you rely on them. Fight. And continue to fight. But the second you believe you will lose," she began.

He looked right at her now. "I'll call you, and you'll end this," he said.

She nodded. Just one short move, her chin jutting out and her head bobbing down. Then she turned swiftly on her foot and left.

John was alone.

He stared down at his hands, up at the force field, then closed his eyes.

He rested his body back against the cell wall. And John started to fight.

Chapter Twelve

Leana'x

She didn't know quite how to describe this. It wasn't that she didn't possess the capacity to put into words what she was experiencing, it was that she didn't have the damn energy. She'd drastically underestimated the cost of having a broken AVA in her mind. She could barely keep track of time, let alone engage in the unending meditation that Na'van kept insisting she try.

It had been a day and a half now, and they were rapidly approaching Artaxan space. But it wasn't easy. Just as predicted, they were facing heavy resistance. Na'van had already informed Leana'x that a man referring to himself as Prince Maqx had sent out a communication on all Coalition lines informing the rest of the galaxy that Leana'x was behind the assassination of the Artaxan Royal Family.

It was yet more goddamn fuel to throw onto the fire.

Leana'x knew for a fact that Na'van had wanted to keep this information to herself, but when the ships had started to track them, that had been impossible.

Leana'x sat in the navigation chair, close beside Na'van as she worked on the primary navigation panel. Na'van didn't speak. She simply concentrated. As for Leana'x, every time it looked as if she was paying too much attention to what Na'van was doing, Na'van would swivel a single eye toward Leana'x and tell her to meditate.

Leana'x couldn't meditate anymore. She couldn't think. She just wanted to... what? Give up? Let herself sink into the fear that had been trying to claim her for the past day and a half?

To be honest, the worst thing Leana'x could do right now was close her mind off to everything that was happening around her and try to meditate. Because every time she did, the weakness slammed into her mind, front and center, and she couldn't escape the damage of holding AVA.

She could barely move her body unassisted anymore.

Suddenly, there was a beep from the console beside her, and just as she swiveled her head to look at it, Na'van snapped up from beside her, swiveled around in a graceful move and slammed her palms against the console. Instantly, the information blinking over the screen embedded in the panel went dark.

Again Leana'x could pick up the unmistakable energy that signified Na'van mentally communicating with the ship.

Despite the fact it had been a day and a half, Leana'x hadn't found out any more about that mysterious process, even though her questions kept mounting.

Na'van wouldn't answer, anyway, and before Leana'x could start to suspect that Na'van was hiding something, she could appreciate Na'van was probably just trying to keep her safe. The last thing Leana'x needed right now was more information. Because every time she learned some new fact, it would always bring with it some new problem, too.

Though Na'van usually kept her expression completely neutral and barely reacted to what she saw coming in over the ship's scanners, suddenly the Light Guard stiffened. It was a barely perceptible move, and Leana'x only picked it up because she'd been concentrating on Na'van with all her might.

Leana'x's stomach clenched of its own accord, and a frown pressed itself across her lips. "What is it?" she asked, her tone breathy.

It took Na'van several seconds to answer. "Move your chair into the center of the room. Place it over the shield generator," Na'van snapped.

Na'van, despite the fact she'd been spending most of the past day and a half trying to evade Coalition ships, had also been simultaneously making changes to the light cruiser – beyond the obvious changes she'd already made to propulsion. One of the first alterations she'd made was to the bridge itself. Na'van was extremely protective, and despite the fact Leana'x was no use to anyone, and certainly didn't need to be on the bridge to help Na'van, Na'van wouldn't let Leana'x out of her sight. So she'd built some kind of modified shield generator and embedded it right into the floor of the bridge. She had to scrounge some of the shielding right out of engineering, but that didn't matter to the Light Guard. All that mattered was keeping Leana'x safe, no matter the costs to the rest of the ship.

When Leana'x didn't react immediately, Na'van twisted around, locked a hand on the back of her chair, then shifted Leana'x into the center of the shield generator. There was a click as Na'van obviously mentally communicated with the ship once more, and a second later, the flickering blue-green shield snapped in place, surrounding Leana'x's chair completely.

She blinked through it as she locked her gaze on the Light Guard. "What's happening?" She couldn't control the fear in her tone.

"We're being tracked by a Coalition strike vessel. They are close," Na'van said.

Leana'x balked. This was the first time in a day and a half that Na'van had ever admitted to the fact they were being tracked, even though Leana'x had seen the security warnings coming over the control panel.

Which meant one thing. The hologram was nervous, so that strike vessel would have to be close.

Suddenly, the ship lurched to the side. No warning. No blaring red alerts. Just a jerk as if the ship had been slapped.

Leana'x blinked hard and instantly tried to shove herself out of her chair, but there was nowhere to go, and she just didn't have the muscular strength to try. Her hands tightened on the armrests as the bridge gave another wobble.

It didn't affect Leana'x in the slightest. Not only was she surrounded by the shield, but the seat she was on was floating. It had its own independent lock with the shield, and even if the ship lost complete gravity and started to barrel roll, it wouldn't affect Leana'x at all.

You know what could affect Leana'x? The complete destruction of the light cruiser.

She'd never seen Na'van act quicker. The hologram darted from console to console, utilizing every skill she had to try to maneuver the ship out of harm's way.

But a second later, a warning alarm finally started to blare. It was pitching, keening, kind of like the warning cry of a hawk.

Sweat slicked across Leana'x's brow, and her heart beat harder in her chest. As soon as it did, this weary, nauseating sensation picked up from her gut and slammed hard into her head. She wobbled on her seat.

Na'van instantly cut her gaze toward her. "Do not fear. I will solve this. Even if I must fight hand-to-hand," she added.

Though fear still assailed Leana'x, despite Na'van's desires, Leana'x did have a moment to appreciate one fact. Though she'd experienced some of Na'van's incredible skills over the past day and a half, she still hadn't seen the Light Guard in combat. She could bet one thing. When she did, it would be a sight to behold. For if the Light Guard was to be believed – and Leana'x had absolutely no reason to doubt her anymore – then she was a weapon specifically designed by the Originals themselves. Leana'x couldn't even begin to imagine the destructive capacity that Na'van was capable of. But something clicked in her head. She didn't want to see it. Because that strike vessel was Coalition. It would be under the false impression that Leana'x was an assassin, and that she had to be tracked down for the Galactic good. But that impression aside, the ship was still Coalition. And the last thing she wanted to see was this Light Guard go to town on it, even if it would keep Leana'x safe.

Leana'x shook her head hard. "We need to find a way to get away from here. We can't engage. We can't afford to spread the Coalitions force's thin—"

"Do not concern yourself with the tactical decisions ahead. You must simply meditate," Na'van said, her voice hard.

Leana'x collapsed in her seat. It wasn't just her weakness – it was the fact that despite AVA in her head, despite her position as Prime, and despite all the power she seemingly had, she was the weakest player in this game.

"Brace yourself," Na'van suddenly snapped.

Leana'x didn't have time. Her shield rippled in intensity, the light now so bright, Leana'x momentarily couldn't see the rest of the bridge.

But while the light could protect her from projectiles, it didn't affect sound. And Leana'x screamed as she heard a massive crunch. The ship shook so violently, what little she could see of the view screen jerked to one side as the consoles below it jerked to the other.

She heard them crack, picked up the unmistakable sound of splintering metal.

Instantly, Na'van blasted forward, slamming a hand toward the console, grabbing it, and bodily holding it against the view screen. As she did, she let a charge of power slice across her hand and spread over the bridge. It was a shield of sorts, and it was just enough to hold the bridge in place.

The warning alarms now didn't just blare through the ship – they practically tore through the metal as they attempted to warn everyone on board just how much shit they were in.

Leana'x panted, her chest punching in and out, and it was enough to push away her fatigue as her eyes pulsed wide.

Her shields dimmed, the immediate attack over.

As they did, she saw the bridge had almost been ripped in half.

There were massive cracks along the floor, up the walls, and across the ceiling. Several pockets of neural wiring had spilled from a broken vent directly above the view screen, and they crackled back and forth, splashing the toxic liquid onto Na'van.

Na'van didn't care. It didn't affect her in the least.

She kept her gaze locked on the view screen as she manipulated the panels.

Leana'x had never been in a more terrifying situation. There was nothing she could do. She was locked against a goddamn chair inside a shield, and though she could see a fraction of the screen, it wasn't enough to know how close or far away they were from danger.

For all she knew, Na'van might have just saved them. Or maybe that strike vessel had just rammed the light cruiser and the Coalition crew aboard were about to transport over.

Her heart didn't just throb in her chest anymore – it barreled around as if it were a ship that had lost its moorings.

Na'van suddenly snapped to the side, shifting toward Leana'x with such a blazing, quick movement, for a second, Leana'x's heart told her Na'van was about to attack.

But that was the last thing the Light Guard was going to do.

She entered the shield protecting Leana'x, and though the shield was one of the strongest the ship could produce, that didn't matter to the Light Guard. Na'van could enter it with ease. As electricity discharged over her body, she wrapped a hand around Leana'x's shoulder and protected Leana'x with the bulk of her back. At the same time, the Light Guard brought up one of her arms, pulsed her hand into a fist, and started to produce her own force field.

The symbols that shifted in and out over the Light Guard's fingers suddenly shifted right off the skin. They started to spin in the air just in front of her fingertips, and the force field the Light Guard was producing tripled and then quadrupled in strength.

It was just in time.

Because suddenly a projectile rammed right through the side of the bridge. It penetrated the hull, and Leana'x's eyes widened as she saw the hard metal nose of an incursion hook stop just several inches from Na'van's back.

Na'van whirled on her foot. Keeping her arm up and keeping the force field pulsing over Leana'x's form, the Light Guard reached around and grabbed the gun from her back. Again, it hadn't been holstered there. But as Na'van's fingers spread wide, Leana'x saw it form in the Light Guard's hand with a snap and flash of light.

Instantly Na'van jolted to the side and started firing.

It was just in time.

A second later, Coalition soldiers started to transport onto the ship.

They were attacking, but Na'van would fight back.

Chapter Thirteen

John Campbell

The ship was under attack.

Jesus Christ, the ship was under attack.

John had been in some pretty terrifying situations before, but this was completely different.

Locked down in the brig with a level X force field keeping him from the rest of the ship, he had no way of figuring out what was happening.

He tried to hope that they would be okay, but a second later, the ship lurched so violently to the side, he was thrown toward the shields. Just before he reached them and could have his face burnt clean off, an impediment force field formed and pushed him back. Obviously the Light Guard hadn't wanted John dying so easily.

The wind was knocked right out of his lungs as he slammed against the floor, rolled, and stopped with his back against the wall.

He had just several seconds to sit there, propped, his

chest rocking back-and-forth as he sucked in breath after breath into his fear-addled body, then it happened again. The ship lurched. Except this time, it was a heck of a lot more violent. He wasn't just thrown to the side, he heard something crack. And that specific metallic groan was a sound that was well-known to anyone who traveled in space.

The hull had just been punctured.

His eyes blasted wide, the skin around them feeling not just as if it would break, but as if it would fall off like rubber bands and twang uselessly against the shield.

John's head didn't have time to tell him he was about to die. Even though it was a foregone conclusion.

Though on an ordinary Coalition ship there'd be somebody guarding the brig in case of a ship-wide alert, this wasn't an ordinary Coalition ship anymore, and though the Light Guard seemed to want to keep him alive, he knew 150% that her priority was Leana'x, just as it should be.

But John was wrong. He wasn't going to die here.

With a groan like a metal mountain being split in half, something punched its way through the ship's hull. As fear tore through him and his heart catapulted at 100 million miles an hour, his training recognized that sound. It was a breach hook. This metal contraption designed to be fired from a Coalition strike vessel. It would have impacted the light cruiser's hull, burrowing right through the metal and locking the strike ship against it so a party could board.

Jesus Christ. *Jesus Christ!*

A Coalition ship had caught up to them. And if John had had any hope before that there were those in the Coalition who didn't suspect Leana'x, this was all the information he needed to conclude he was wrong. The Coalition wouldn't send a strike team with a goddamn breach hook unless they wanted Leana'x dead or alive.

The ship lurched again, and John once more was thrown toward the shields.

They were still in operation, and so too should be the impediment field that would block him from that blazing field of electricity.

It wasn't in effect.

John almost touched the shields.

Almost.

But at the very last minute just as he could feel his cheeks begin to burn, the force field itself turned off. Because the walls around the brig cracked.

John was in his armor. And though that wouldn't have been enough to protect him from the modified force field, it could produce its own atmosphere.

Which was precisely what he needed as the brig was breached.

A massive crack formed down one wall, and he suddenly saw the brig depressurize as everything that wasn't tied down was sucked toward the hole.

He was thrown from his feet, but at the last moment, he forced his armor to make a magnetic lock against the floor. His feet slammed against it, and as they did, he gave his armor a mental command to snap his helmet into place.

John stared from the huge crack in the brig wall, then darted his head over his shoulder, locking his full attention on the door out of the brig.

It was still closed. Though that was a technicality. The metal was warped. It looked as if somebody with huge destructive capacity had just picked up the reinforced metal and crumpled it like paper.

John took a step toward it. Though his right leg was strong, his left leg wobbled. Wait, no, wobbled wasn't the right term. It jerked as if it wanted to make him move faster.

No. John hadn't forgotten the fact that the Replacement James Jones' mind was still infecting his consciousness. The immediacy of this situation might have pushed James back for now, but with a quick, involuntary curl of the left side of John's mouth, it was clear that the Admiral was back.

"Not now. You bastard, not now. Not when she needs us so much," John managed to say with only half his mouth.

"Now is the perfect time," his mouth replied back as he momentarily lost control of his voice and James Jones took hold.

John didn't have the time to stand there and stare at the door in complete fear as he waited for Jones to strike the final blow and fully take over his body. No. John could hear voices. Screams. Shouts. Shit, an incursion team. They were headed this way.

John had absolutely no intention of ever working with Admiral Jones. The Replacement wanted one thing and one thing alone. The complete and total destruction of John's consciousness. Worse. He wanted to use John's hands to snap Leana'x's throat – and there was no way John was ever going to let that happen. John would wring his own throat before he let Admiral Jones go through with that dark desire.

But right now John could appreciate one fact. If he had any hope of getting out of here and facing the Coalition team outside the door without dying, then, in a way, they needed to work together. Or at least, Jones needed to give John back control of his body long enough to make a difference.

John wasn't going to beg, though. He was never gonna frigging beg. But as he made another step toward the doorway, it was smoother this time. He just hoped that Jones, however twisted and freaking broken, could appreciate that the only way out of here was together.

A second later, John heard exactly what he expected to – the sound of a directed laser against metal.

They were trying to breach the door.

He took up a defensive position, getting ready, his back slicked with sweat that wouldn't dry, his mouth full of the bitter, iron taste of belly-crushing fear.

Then there was a crack. Was there a scream, too? One that was cut short?

John's brow was slicked with sweat as he jerked back just in time. Something slammed against the door and it blasted inward.

He expected to see an incursion team. That's not what he got.

He got the Light Guard, with Leana'x thrown over the hologram's shoulder.

John balked and immediately threw himself forward, spreading a hand out toward Leana'x. She was limp like a ragdoll, and the mere sight set John's heart pounding like a hammer to an anvil.

But he never reached Leana'x. The Light Guard shifted to the side, brought up her hand so quickly, John's armor had no chance to track it, and she caught his wrist.

She didn't say a word.

She didn't have to. Realization slammed into John. He had no right to touch Leana'x anymore – not considering what was still in his head. He swallowed hard and swiveled his head toward the door. "What's going on out there?"

"We have been boarded by a Coalition strike vessel. We

must leave the ship, take over the strike vessel, and use it to get to Artaxan Prime."

John stared in shock. "Wait? What? We can't take over that ship – they're my—"

"Before you attest to the fact they're your colleagues, remember that you have a far more important mission to complete right now. And anyone or anything that gets in its way must be treated the same – as an adversary. You yourself pointed out that there's no way to know how many people in the Coalition Academy were part of the conspiracy to kill the Artaxan Royal Family."

John opened his mouth, but then he heard footsteps. John didn't have time to react. Na'van did. Without even turning over her shoulder, she produced a gun from somewhere and seamlessly fired through the gap in the door. There was a clunk as a heavy, armored body hit the ground.

John's eyes blasted wide, but before he could demand to know whether Na'van had killed that Coalition soldier, she simply made eye contact and shook her head as if she'd already known what he'd been about to ask. She looked right at him again, those little electronic cogs in her eyes spinning around faster than ever before as if what she would say next would count the most. "Commander, I know you have loyalty for your Coalition. Which they deserve. But right now—"

He acted first. He rounded both hands into fists, though they weren't nearly as hard as whenever the Admiral took control. "I get it. I know," he said, voice raspy, "right now, Leana'x is my priority. Because without Leana'x... none of this will exist anyway," he managed.

Na'van continued to make direct eye contact until she slowly nodded, that regal, in-control quality back to her movements. She turned swiftly on her foot and headed out the door.

She didn't have to look at her targets. She didn't seemingly have to track them with her head and eyes. Her arm would just move of its own accord, whatever strange but powerful gun gripped in her fingers firing off pinpoint perfect blasts that would take out the Coalition soldiers boarding the ship.

John shouldn't have to point out he'd never seen anything like it. For good reason. Because he could not allow himself to forget that this Light Guard came from the time of the Originals.

... This wasn't the time to point it out, but a part of John still reeled at the fact that the Force and the Originals existed at all. He'd never heard about the Force growing up and had only learned about them recently through his security privilege as a Coalition Commander. As for the Originals, if it weren't for the Chief Engineer on board the *Hercules*, he would never have heard of those races, either.

But now the Originals and the Force – races that existed long, long before the modern galaxy – now held the future of the Coalition in their grasps, the future of the Milky Way, too.

It didn't seem right. That's not what progress promised. Progress promised you would always go up, never down. But the fact remained that the Coalition didn't even begin to have the kind of technology that the Originals did. Which the Light Guard only served to underline as she continued to easily push her way through the vessel.

There wasn't a thing John had to do. More to the point, there wasn't a thing she would let him do. With snapped orders, she told him to stay close by her side and not to act.

He knew exactly what she was afraid of, and to be honest, he was afraid of the same thing too. After all, Leana'x was right there. Right there. All he would have to do was take two swift steps to her side, and he could latch his hands around—

He suddenly shook his head, the move so powerful his armor gave him a warning blip to point out he was close to muscle strain.

He ignored it.

Goddamn Admiral Jones. John could never allow himself to forget the fact that the Admiral was still there – always there, lurking in the background of John's mind, ready to attack.

Just waiting.

So John wouldn't allow himself to look at Leana'x.

John could appreciate that the Light Guard was constrained by the fact she had to keep both John and Leana'x safe. If that hadn't been a priority, John could easily imagine that she would've already decimated the strike team and taken over the vessel. He could predict that she could probably move through matter, if not transport completely. After all, technically she was a hologram.

... That was a big technicality, wasn't it? Because she was definitely unlike any other holographic technology he'd ever seen. Though ever since the Circle trader incident it was becoming known to the Coalition that solid-state holograms and the technology to create them already existed in the Milky Way, the Light Guard was something on a completely different level.

She was a true weapon. And it made John shudder to think just how easily she could go against the Coalition, if she so chose to.

But right now he had to remind himself that this wasn't going against the Coalition, this was trying to save the Milky Way.

So he remained in lock step behind her as she pushed through the light cruiser.

It quickly became apparent to John that this Coalition strike team wasn't playing around. They had pinned the ship from two places, practically destroying it. Though it was usual Coalition style to try to save the vessel if you knew the combatants on board weren't going to put up much of a fight, this was brutal.

And it made John's back chill. Because it told him one thing.

What... what if more assassins were onboard the strike vessel?

He didn't have time to articulate that out loud. Suddenly a massive chunk of wall paneling beside him blasted outward. But before it could sail into the Light Guard and strike Leana'x, John got there first. He sailed forward, brought his fist up and slammed it into the paneling, punching it right out of the way.

He landed on his foot, pivoted hard, and watched the Light Guard take on two fully armed mech soldiers.

Mech suit soldiers were half way between ordinary armor and full battle armor. A relatively new addition to the Coalition Army, they were what you used in pitched land battle. They were huge, the Mech suits standing at about an average of ten feet tall each.

They were as wide as Earth rhinoceroses, too, and just as goddamn violent.

With no warning, they threw themselves at the Light Guard.

She, however, didn't need a warning.

John didn't even have the time to throw himself toward her in the hopes he could help. With Leana'x still locked over her shoulder, Na'van simply swiped her arm to the side. As she did, those unusual tattoos that usually remained on her fingertips swiped forward, actually removing themselves from the skin as if they were small devices.

As they did, he heard an unusual hum pick up through the air. It had precisely half a second and then it created a shield.

One that spun in a circle in front of the Light Guard and then shoved forward. It blasted into the Mech suits, slamming them back into the wall panel they'd just erupted from.

There was such a grinding of metal, it sounded as if in one single blow the Light Guard managed to completely obliterate the Mech suits.

One thing was for sure, they didn't get up.

"What the hell was that?" John managed.

The Light Guard, suffice to say, didn't have time to answer.

She spun hard on her foot and continued forward, running now.

John knew for a fact that not too many strike vessels had goddamn Mech suits. Which pointed out yet again there was a high damn possibility they were dealing with assassins.

Shit.

Even if John had complete control of his mind, this would be the worst possible situation.

It brought up that question again – just how far would John go against his own people – against the Coalition – to keep Leana'x safe?

The answer came right around the corner as a contingent of soldiers rushed toward them.

Though there were three ahead, John picked up the slightest shift in energy behind him, and his instincts warned him just in time that three more were transporting just behind him.

He whirled on his foot. He brought up his fists. That's all he had.

They had guns. Pulse disruptors, to be precise. Extremely violent weaponry that was only used when it had to be. The kind of stuff you cracked out when you knew you were dealing with the hardest Barbarian assassins out there.

But John wasn't a Barbarian assassin, for God's sake. Neither was Leana'x.

He had just enough time to launch forward, push up into a jump, and slam his fist against the closest soldier, then the Light Guard did the rest.

She didn't even have to shift her position. She just fired. Six blasts. Faster than a goddamn computer could. Heck, faster than the targeting array of a heavy cruiser.

She was beyond anything he'd ever seen. And, fortunately, she was beyond anything the soldiers expected. With six heavy clunks, they struck the ground.

John took a shaky step backward, his breath trapped in his chest.

He had just enough time to pivot on his foot and make eye contact with the Light Guard until he heard the unmistakable sound of pounding footfall rushing toward him once more.

"Duck," he managed.

The Light Guard did not duck.

Instead, in a swift move, she took a strong step toward John and brought her arm up. Now those tattoos that had once been embedded in her fingers were spinning around her arm, creating some kind of electrical discharge. It was enough to produce a massive force field that locked in place around them just in time.

For a second later, a massive discharge of energy erupted down the corridor, blasting into the walls, pulling off the paneling, and completely obliterating the neural wire within with an eerie hiss and the unmistakable scent of burnt biological matter.

If it weren't for the blast shield embedded in John's helmet, the sheer brightness of that attack would've burnt off his retinas.

He'd never seen anything like it. Because the Coalition strike team were cracking out weaponry he'd never even heard of.

"Come," the Light Guard said simply.

She sauntered forward. No, sauntered wasn't the right word. There was no arrogance in her move – there was no arrogance in her anywhere. She wasn't like a recruit who thought she was better than everyone else. For the love of God, though he'd already pointed this out, she was from the time of the Originals. And she was better than everyone else.

Maybe it was a fact the strike vessel team was starting to appreciate, because they didn't throw soldiers at them anymore.

They hung back.

They would be planning. In John's mind's eye, he could see them gathered around on the bridge, sweat slicking their brows, hearts beating in their chests, but fists curled.

They wouldn't be giving up.

To them, they were saving the galaxy. To John, they were trying to destroy it.

The Light Guard led John toward the hatch in the back of the ship.

There was a problem, though. A big honking great problem. It was an incursion hook, to be precise. It had obliterated part of the hatch wall. If it weren't for the shield crackling in place over it, the entire ship would've depressurized and they all would've been sucked out into space.

John just had enough time to clench his teeth and hiss through them.

Jesus Christ, this strike team were beyond serious. They were utilizing the kind of techniques you used against your worst enemy – not somebody who could be innocent.

Which told him one thing, right? In these guys' heads, John and Leana'x couldn't be innocent.

There was no way.

So there'd be no reasoning with them.

... Though it hurt just to think this, though it goddamn goaded his heart, he had to agree with the Light Guard. The only way that they were going to get through this was to take over that strike ship.

As that realization sunk through his heart, he lifted his chin up, he settled his gaze, and he kept close behind the Light Guard.

"What's the plan?" John asked.

The Light Guard took several seconds to answer. Then she pointed one of her elegant hands toward the massive incursion hook. "I will remove that, then we will take over the strike ship. You will remain by my side. You will not reach for Leana'x. No matter what happens. Do you understand?"

John clenched his teeth.

Ever since this frantic battle had begun, he'd barely heard the Admiral. He wasn't an idiot, though. The Admiral was still there, lurking in the depths of John's consciousness. And the bastard would be biding his time.

But right now, for whatever reason, he was letting John do what John needed to do.

So John made easy eye contact with the Light Guard. He nodded.

She didn't wait.

Somehow, even though Leana'x was still propped over her shoulder, the Light Guard shifted forward, brought up her free hand, and locked it on the massive incursion hook in the side of the wall.

It was being protected by its own force field and a combination of the light cruiser's hull shields – their last-ditch attempt to ensure pressurization in the ship.

Even one of those Mech suits from before wouldn't have been able to bodily shift the incursion hook, let alone settle a hand past its massive shields.

John shouldn't really need to point out that the Light Guard had no trouble. With a dull click, he heard the light cruiser's depressurization shields turn off.

Several seconds later, the Light Guard bothered to hiss, "Prepare yourself for depressurization. Ensure your armor is creating atmosphere."

Fortunately for John, his helmet was solidly in place, and as the hatch depressurized with a hiss, his lungs didn't pop.

John had no idea how the Light Guard did it, but with Leana'x still propped over one shoulder, and only one hand rested on the incursion hook, somehow the hologram pushed the hook out. Not all the way. She didn't need to push it back into the strike ship completely. Just enough to make a gap so they could push through.

There were countless reasons why this shouldn't be happening. Countless countermeasures and technical defenses in place to ensure someone couldn't just push an incursion hook out. None of that mattered.

On the other side of the incursion hook was the specialized outer bay of the strike ship. It wasn't only where the incursion hook was deployed and controlled from, but it was where the strike team would transport from. As the Light Guard shoved the incursion hook bodily out of the way, John started to hear screams. From the exact desperate pitch of them, it was pretty obvious that people were terrified out of their minds.

He didn't blame them.

As soon as the Light Guard had pushed the hook sufficiently clear to catch a glimpse of the incursion bay, the entire room lit up with blasting beams of light as the crew within attempted to repel boarders.

Though John's heart was beating at a million miles an hour and trying to tell him that he was seconds from dying, die he did not.

The Light Guard didn't seem to have a care in the world as she sauntered right out of the hole she'd made, Leana'x still propped over one shoulder. That strange shield she'd created was still in place, and fortunately for John, it protected the both of them as every soldier in the incursion bay fired everything they damn well had at him. But it wasn't enough.

John's heart didn't just beat in his chest anymore. He was pretty damn sure it was trying to travel out of his rib cage and beyond light speed.

He had no idea what the Light Guard was going to do. Yeah, he'd made his peace with the fact that this – saving Leana'x no matter the costs – was the only thing they could do right now. But he was still a part of the Coalition. He still lived, breathed, and damn well existed for the peace the

Coalition created through the Milky Way. He'd joined them to make a difference. And all of that loyalty swelled in his head right now as he wondered just how far the Light Guard was willing to go. Because if she decided to go all the way – and completely rid the strike vessel of resistance, killing every soldier in sight, there wasn't a damn thing anyone would be able to do to stop her.

... But she didn't do it. Why bother? With whatever fancy force field she was producing with her arm, there wasn't a thing the soldiers in the bay could do.

Yet. They kept trying. They were just as dutiful toward the Coalition as John was, after all. But even their best efforts didn't matter.

The Light Guard strode right between them, forcefully striking down anyone who got in her way, but not killing them.

She made it toward the door on the opposite side of the room. It was heavily protected by the kind of force field that should make a torpedo stop in its tracks.

The Light Guard? She didn't bother to go through the door. She pivoted on her foot just at the last moment, shoved her hand into the floor next to the door, and ripped off a massive section of plating. She shoved a hand into the exposed wiring and ripped it out with the force and speed of an Arctic Fox digging for its prey. After several frantic, un-trackable movements, the force field in front of the door just flickered out, the tech that had been producing it now completely obliterated.

Though John was amazed by what was happening, he didn't let himself lose track of where he was, even for a second. He knew if he dared to venture too far away from the Light Guard, he'd be toast. The only thing keeping him alive was his proximity to her. And the second he was dumb enough to step away from her, was the second this would be all over.

"Come," the Light Guard said simply as she swiped a hand forward, shoved her fist against the now unshielded door, and opened it a crack. She swept her foot up and kicked the door, and it spun out into the corridor.

There were more soldiers waiting outside, but this time they didn't attack. No, they turned tail and started to retreat.

Thank God. *Finally,* John thought to himself, relief flooding through his gut. Whoever was in charge of this ship had obviously realized there was no goddamn way they were gonna fight the Light Guard, and retreat was the only option.

Or at least, that's what John's training wanted to tell him. A second later, the Light Guard ticked her head to the side with a robotic move. John was just to the side of her, and it gave him all the vantage he needed to see her eyes widen with a pulse of shock. Her lips stiffened.

"What is it?" John managed.

"They have just initiated the self-destruct on this vessel. I must destroy the system to save this ship," she added with a quick hiss.

Though he knew her priority was to get to the bridge and end this ship's resistance in one swift move, suddenly the Light Guard jolted to the side. John wasn't particularly familiar with this specific design of strike vessel, but almost all Coalition ships had similar attributes. He could tell the bridge would be at the front of the vessel, and engineering usually was right in the middle, in the most protected place it could be.

And that's where the Light Guard headed now. She

moved so damn quickly that John could only just catch up, and even then it was a struggle.

He was no longer thinking of Admiral Jones, to be honest. And as he streamed down the corridor, following the Light Guard, it was almost as if he'd forgotten the beast was still lurking in the depths of his consciousness. Admiral Jones? Yeah. He hadn't forgotten. He was waiting for an opportunity that would come soon.

Chapter Fourteen

Leana'x

THIS... SHE... COULDN'T EVEN BEGIN TO UNDERSTAND what was happening.

Though ever since becoming the Prime Queen of the Artaxan Protectorate Leana'x hadn't exactly led a safe life, she'd experienced nothing compared to this.

The smell of destruction that laced the air. The burnt metals, the singed flesh, the cracked and convulsing neural wire.

The sight of the crumpled walls and doors and devices around her.

This was the stuff of nightmares.

No amount of training at the Academy could prepare one for this. For the visceral experience of destruction.

But there was one thing she could be thankful for. The Light Guard was keeping Leana'x safe without demonstrably hurting anyone else.

And yet that didn't even matter now, did it?

Because the crew of this ship were so goddamn intent

on killing Leana'x and John, that they seemed to be prepared to sacrifice everything – including their vessel and their own lives – to get that task done.

Leana'x couldn't... she couldn't begin to understand why.

She'd harbored the foolish hope that the Coalition would see through Prince Maqx's stupid lies. What about the crew of the *Hercules*? What about Captain Chan and the Chief Engineer? She'd conversed with them, they'd witnessed her transformation, and they'd been there when she'd almost been assassinated three times. Wouldn't they have raised their voices? Wouldn't they have added reason to the fear the Coalition had? And shouldn't that reason have won out?

It was too late now. *It was too late for hope.*

The conclusion was forgone.

If Prince Maqx and the other assassins couldn't kill Leana'x with their own hands, they'd get the Coalition to do it for them.

Leana'x... she wanted to connect to AVA now more than anything. She wanted to rely on the Intelligence, hope that it could tell her how to get out of this situation.

But there was nothing in Leana'x's mind. Nothing but a cold fog that seemed to be wrapping further around her with every second. It was the kind of cold fog that could only promise one thing – death.

Because Leana'x was dying.

There was no denying that.

Since she'd been plucked out of that pod in the palace, Leana'x had been slowly falling apart.

And now there was no hope.

Because even if the Light Guard could perform a miracle, save this ship, acquire it, and fly out of here, there'd still be no way to get Leana'x to the throne room in time.

The conclusion was forgone.

Forgone.

There was nothing she could do.

If the Light Guard weren't currently desperately attempting to stop the self-destruct, she'd probably take the time to tell Leana'x to remain calm.

But how the hell were you meant to remain calm when your entire world was crumbling before your feet?

The cold fog continued to swirl around her, denser now. Sapping all the last of her heat until Leana'x lay limp.

She waited.

But she didn't know what for. The end? For someone to save her?

Or for Leana'x to finally save herself?

...

Admiral Jones

Chaos. Bedlam. It was exactly what the Admiral needed. He would smile if he could. He knew there was no point. The less he controlled John now, and the more he allowed the fool to be drawn in by the fear and desperation of the situation, the easier it would be to control him when it mattered most. And the Admiral would only need one second. One second to find a weapon, to fire it at Leana'x. And finally, finally this mess would all be over.

But first, he would have to distract the Light Guard.

Maybe the self-destruct would do that.

The Admiral had known of the Light Guard through his connection to the Force, but even he had been surprised by the Light Guard's efficiency and pure destructive capacity.

Though the Admiral didn't have a pure connection to the Force anymore, he could appreciate that it was critical that the Light Guard die.

She could not be allowed to live, even once Leana'x was killed. If the Light Guard were allowed to fall into the Coalition's clutches, they might be able to understand the technology that created her. And if they got desperate enough, and she got desperate enough, they may learn how to create Light Guards of their own.

No. The Admiral would have to act. But that was a task for later. For now all he had to do was wait.

The Light Guard reached engineering.

There was heavy resistance, possibly even heavier than in the incursion room. It was clear the crew of this ship were regretting the decision to attack. Though the Admiral wasn't in charge of John's senses, he swore he could still smell the collective fear of the crew. If the Admiral had been in his own body, he would have rejoiced at the sensation. This was the type of desperation that the Force had lived for. The exquisite fear of biological creatures when they realize their lives are about to be taken from them forever and there was nothing they could damn well do about it.

But the Admiral had to remind himself that the Light Guard was determined to save Leana'x; she wasn't here to destroy the ship.

She would need it.

How many hours did Leana'x have now? 12? 10? Less than that?

Of their own accord, John Campbell's eyes darted toward Leana'x.

She wasn't moving. She hadn't moved since he'd seen her in the brig.

She wasn't dead, though. Just what? Knocked out? Too weak to even remain conscious anymore?

It was a tantalizing prospect. But even though the Admiral could just wait for Leana'x to die naturally, he would not be denied the satisfaction of overcoming John and using the fool's own body to kill her.

It was poetic, after all. The Admiral also had to maximize every chance that AVA would transfer to his body, not Prince Maxq's.

The Light Guard soon got irritated at the resistance the crew were putting up, and she just blasted them away. No. She didn't kill them. Using the modified shield that was produced by the strange markings over her fingers, she sent out a huge impediment blast that blew everyone off their feet and slammed them into the walls. It didn't matter if they were in sophisticated armor. They were all blasted back. It gave the Light Guard the opportunity she needed to stream forward, bring her foot up, and plant it against the engineering bay doors. She kicked them clean off. She had so much power that they blasted inward into engineering, sailed through the large bay, and slammed into the shielded engine cores on the opposite side of the room. Fortunately, she didn't kick the door hard enough that the metal sailed right through the cores – they were far too protected for that.

She gave herself all the distraction she needed as she strode in, though. The crew inside scuttled to get out of her way.

Though the Admiral still couldn't read Campbell's thoughts, it was damn clear that the Commander was willing to do everything he could to help the Light Guard.

The Light Guard needed no help.

She strode right over to a panel near the engineering cores, locked a hand against it, half closed her eyes, and shifted her focus. As she did, the color of her eyes changed.

The engineering crew behind were not willing to give up their vessel yet.

The Admiral was aware as John pivoted hard on his foot, as his eyes blasted wide in fear. "They're going to—" he had time to say.

The Commander didn't have time to finish his warning.

The Chief Engineer sabotaged her own engine.

A pulse of blinding light shifted through the room. Fortunately for the Admiral, it wasn't the full might of the cores suddenly blasting into main engineering. No. It was the shields that held them in place going into a critical cascade.

Suddenly the loudest alert possible began to blare through the ship.

"Critical overload of quantum engine cores. Irreversible self-destruct initiated. All crew are to evacuate the vessel. Two minutes until the complete destruction of this ship. One minute and 59 seconds," the alarm continued to count down.

The Light Guard stopped what she was doing.

She turned hard on her foot.

She faced the Commander.

Or did she face the Admiral?

As her eyes focused, it quickly became clear she was trying to look right through John's eyes to something further in.

She suddenly yanked a hand forward, locked it on John's collar, and drew him close with an easy move. "You will save her. You will overcome the Admiral. You will get her off this ship. Do you understand?"

The Admiral tried to answer back.

But John got there first.

The bastard opened his own lips and replied, "I understand. But what will you—"

"I will buy you the time you need to do that." With that, the Light Guard handed Leana'x over, the Prime Queen of the Artaxan Protectorate.

The Admiral's heart could have exploded, if he'd had one. His mind could've raced, his breathing should have restricted.

But he wasn't in control of John's body. Not yet.

But soon. Goddamn soon.

Because the moment the Admiral had been waiting for finally occurred.

John brought his arms up and accepted Leana'x.

It was then that the Admiral realized she was awake. Either she'd just woken, or she'd been in a meditative state the entire time. As she was handed over to John, she locked her desperate gaze on him.

As for John? The Admiral could feel as his brow twitched down low, his eyes opened wide, and a terrified smile creased his lips. "Leana'x," he managed in a hoarse voice.

"Go. No more time," the Light Guard commanded as she shoved a hand into John's shoulder and pushed him back.

She never stopped looking at John's eyes, though. And it was now more than clear that she was searching for any trace of the Admiral.

He was here.

And he was waiting.

For the opportunity that was coming.

The Light Guard darted forward.

Nearly all of the engineering crew had already run out of the blasted open main doors, the destruction of their ship forgone.

So there was no one to stop the Light Guard as she suddenly jumped forward. She transported. Right through the critically malfunctioning shields and into the engine core.

The Admiral almost wanted to regain control over John's body just to watch what would happen as the Light Guard was torn apart on the molecular level. It was clear the idiot intended to use the last energy of her body to buy the shields more time.

But it didn't matter how much time the Light Guard bought Leana'x. Her life was about to end.

...

Leana'x

This... it couldn't be happening. God. It couldn't be happening. But it was. Her life and quite possibly the lives of everyone in the galaxy were slipping through her hands.

And there was nothing she could do.

She'd never been weaker. She couldn't move her legs. Even if John dropped her and she had the chance to run away, she wouldn't be able to take it.

John....

She could see his face. The way his cheeks were so heavily lined it looked as if they'd been carved from gnarled wood.

And the focus in his eyes. He wouldn't look at her. Almost as if he wouldn't dare allow himself to make eye contact. If he did that, was he worried that the Admiral inside his brain would take control?

John....

God. She would do anything to save him, but there wasn't a thing she could do.

It took John several seconds to move.

The Light Guard had just sacrificed herself by jumping into the engine cores, and for a few seconds, John stood there, wasting precious time as he stared at the cores, his eyes wide.

But that would be when Leana'x realized it wasn't him staring at the engine.

It was the Admiral.

She was aware of her heart, her breath, the sweat slicking between her shoulders and fingers. She didn't care about that. Every single sense she had she locked on John.

And she waited. Waited for what she knew would happen. Because John wouldn't give in to the Admiral, would he? Leana'x had never met a stronger man.

Come on, he couldn't give in to the Admiral.

It took John several seconds before he managed to pivot on his foot. The move was hard. Held in his arms, Leana'x could tell how rigid he had to make his muscles just to change his position, let alone throw himself forward.

As for his jaw, it was clenched as hard as a vice.

"Come on, come on," he begged himself under his breath.

James stared as he finally managed to take a single step forward, then another.

It was clear he was in the battle for his life. Or at least, hers.

There was no amount of training that could prepare someone for what was happening in John's head. For the love of God, he had a Replacement mind in his consciousness, trying to tear him down from the inside out.

Leana'x wanted to help. She tried to reach a hand up to him again, but once more he asked her in a crippling voice to stop.

So she just lay there in his arms, staring. Waiting to either be killed or saved.

Torture. *This was torture.*

If Leana'x ever actually lived through this, she would never face torture as bad as this.

The inability to act.

Being at the complete whims of others as you waited for them to dictate your fate.

But worse. Much, much worse. Being incapable of saving those you cared about as you watched them fall to pieces right before your very eyes.

Total, heart-wrenching, soul-destroying torture.

And the torture wouldn't end yet.

...

Commander Campbell

No.

This couldn't be happening.

This couldn't goddamn be happening.

The protection of Leana'x was now down to John.

And the Admiral?

Sure, he'd kept quiet during this entire battle. But now that bastard reared his ugly head and fought with everything he had.

Leana'x stared at John's face as he held her aloft and ran down the corridor outside of engineering.

He'd never seen her eyes wider.

He'd never seen so much concentration.

It was almost... as if she needed to see the moment he snapped.

But John wasn't going to snap.

"Just a little longer. Just a little longer," he whispered under his breath. It wasn't for her benefit; it was for his.

He just had to hold out against the Admiral for a little longer.

But it was the most brutal battle that John had ever faced.

For the Admiral was now fighting him on every front.

John almost lost control of his left hand. The fingers pulsed in and out and crunched hard against Leana'x's back.

She shivered, staring down at his shoulder then up at his face, the fear finally starting to dilate her pupils.

"I'm okay. I'm okay. I'm okay," he repeated to himself like a mantra.

She didn't say a word. She just watched him. And in her eyes he saw that somber sadness she'd been staring at him with since the moment she'd found out he'd been possessed.

He couldn't look at it. If he stared too long at the tears trickling down her cheeks, he'd be distracted.

And allow himself to be distracted? And the Admiral would just rush in.

You can do this. You have training. You have a disciplined mind. For God's sake, you have a disciplined mind, John kept repeating to himself as he streamed down the corridors.

The self-destruct countdown still echoed over the loudspeakers.

A minute.

One goddamn minute until the destruction of this entire ship.

There would be no hope. No salvation. No last-ditch miracle.

John needed to get Leana'x off this ship.

That was the only way.

He rounded a corner, only to face a combat soldier.

John didn't hesitate.

He couldn't, could he?

Just as the guy brought his gun up, John pivoted to the side, dropped down low, and kicked, slamming the back of his armored boot against the guy's leg.

The man buckled forward, slammed against the floor, and lost his grip on his gun. It skidded down the hallway.

John didn't make a go for it. Nor did he finish the kill. Do that, and this guy wouldn't have a hope of getting off this ship.

Instead, John just put on a burst of speed and continued running.

From his knowledge of Coalition strike ship design, he knew the escape pods would be close by. Sure enough, as he angled his way toward the outer sections of this deck, he finally found one of the corridors where they were located.

Fortunately, there weren't too many crew left on this deck, and they were so rattled, they couldn't put up a fight.

By the time he finally came streaming around the corner, there was only two engineering staff to contend with. And they were so shocked, there was nothing they could do to stop John as he barreled by. He kicked the both of them right into a waiting escape pod, slammed his hand down on the panel beside it, and watched as the hatch door closed before they could scramble to their feet.

They stared at him with open eyes as the pod disengaged from the ship and flew away.

Leana'x hadn't said a word until now.

She'd just been watching him with her beautiful luminescent irises.

But now John jerked to a stop. Right in front of an open hatch. All he had to do was throw Leana'x inside, activate the pod, and save her.

That's all he had to do.

But at the last moment, just when her salvation was in sight, the Admiral started to fight back.

John could feel his desperation. The anger, too. The vile hatred. It was on a level John had never experienced. He'd heard before that Replacement technology was broken, that it led to fractured minds. Now he experienced it.

But no matter how fractured and broken the Admiral was, he still had enough directed will to fight like a cornered wild animal.

"John?" Leana'x said through a shaking breath as she brought a hand up and tried to latch it on John's helmet.

At the last moment, he jerked his head to the side. "Don't," he said in a strangled voice.

Tears shimmered in her eyes as her fingers stopped several centimeters from his jaw.

She let her hand drop.

And she seemed to wait.

Obviously she knew what was happening in John's head.

She didn't beg for her life. She just watched him, more tears streaking down her cheeks.

And it was the tears that did it.

To think, once upon a time he hated this woman. Now there was nothing he wouldn't do to keep her safe.

Nothing.

He let that promise to himself spread through his head, and it was all he needed to finally do it.

He shifted forward, placed her down in the pod, stood back, then walked outside.

Her eyes blasted even wider now as she realized what was happening. "You're not coming? The ship's going to explode. John, you need to get in here. John!"

The self-destruct was still counting down in the background.

He took another step back. "Just promise me you'll hold on a little longer," he said through a choked voice as he stared at her and finally his own tears touched his cheeks. "Promise me you'll find some way of keeping yourself safe without the throne room. If anyone can do it, it's you, Leana'x."

He took one more step back.

"No, John. Please, John," she begged as she reached a hand toward him.

He stared at her, the most somber smile he'd ever given pressing across his lips. "I'm sorry, Leana'x. It's... it's the only way," he managed. Then he felt another wave of sickness slam through him as the Admiral tried to take control again.

John forced himself to take a step back from the escape pod doors.

As he did, he brought up a hand and clutched it over one side of his face, pressing his palm against his left eye so hard, he started to see stars.

"John. Please," she tried. But Leana'x still couldn't use her legs, and all she could do was try to crawl forward.

John had a moment.

A moment where he almost lost control.

She reached a hand out toward him, and his left hand wanted to grab it, pull her in, and snap her goddamn neck.

His eyes started to twitch. His jaw began to snap to the left and right.

Out of the corner of his eye, he could see tears streaking down her cheeks as she shook there on the spot. "John. Please—"

The Admiral tried with all his might. All his goddamn might to tear John's last vestige of control from his body.

But John held on.

Just long enough.

"Just get out of here. I'm sorry. Leana'x, I'm sorry," he managed, and with that, he finally jerked to the side, slammed his thumb against the panel on the wall, and closed the escape pod hatch.

It sliced in front of his hand, just as his left hand jerked out to hold the door in place.

But Admiral Jones wasn't quick enough.

John stared at Leana'x, and she stared back through the tiny portal window of the hatch.

Then with a hiss and the unmistakable white blast of atmosphere discharging from the side of the ship, her pod ejected.

And John?

He got ready for the fight for his life, or maybe it was his death.

He screamed. The bellow pitched from his throat. Problem was, it didn't come from him. He didn't have vocal control right now – the Admiral did. And John heard as the loudest, most violent scream he'd ever given echoed down the hallway.

He also brought up his left hand, balled it into such a tight fist, his armor started to blare alarms in his helmet, and punched the wall. One beat then another, as if the Admiral wanted to tear right through the paneling, right out through the ship, and try to make a last-ditch grab for Leana'x.

She was gone.

She was safe.

Or at least, she was safe from John.

"She's still going to die. Idiot. She's still going to die," John said to himself, the Admiral taking momentary control of John's voice.

"Shut up, bastard," John snapped back.

"She's got hours. Hours until the burden of AVA tears through her mind anyway. All you've done here is deny me the pleasure of doing it myself—"

"I said shut up, bastard," John bellowed.

He wrenched his hand back from the wall, pivoted on his foot, and tried to run down the corridor, but at the last moment, the Admiral got control over the left side of his body.

John fell, armor thumping against the floor and echoing down the corridor.

The blaring alarm of the self-destruct still echoed through the halls. Far off in some of the other corridors, John could hear more escape pods detaching.

The crew were evacuating.

John?

He stood his ground. Or at least, he sat his ground. And as the Admiral tried to punch to his feet, John just reached forward with his right hand and increased the structural integrity of his fingers, then plunged them into the floor. He held onto the warped metal for dear life as the Admiral tried to pull John's body back.

John would not be moved.

He heard the final countdown initiate.

10 seconds to self-destruct. Nine.

"There's no point in killing us both, *fool*," the Admiral spat with John's lips.

John didn't even bother to reply.

This was the only way.

True... Leana'x would be on her own. But the Replacement Admiral Jones would finally be dead, and the doorway in his head to the Force would go with him.

So John held on.

Eight seconds to self-destruct.

The Admiral fought harder. So vicious. It was like having a laser being turned against the inside of John's mind.

Blood began to pool out of his right nostril, and his eyes flickered back-and-forth as if someone was beating him repetitively on the back of his skull.

But he didn't give up. He didn't let go.

He never surrendered.

The Admiral's screams were incoherent now.

No words. Just guttural aggression.

Six seconds.

The Admiral tried harder. He threw himself against the last of John's psychic defenses.

Five seconds.

Everything the Admiral had, he used against John.

And John started to slip.

Three seconds.

Finally, the Admiral gained full control.

One second.

But it was too late.

The end of Ava Episode Three. This story is concluded in Ava Episode Four, so pick it up today.

Sign up for the Odette C. Bell newsletter at
www.odettecbell.com/pages/newsletter
You will receive two complete series as a thank you.
Thank you for reading!
Head to www.odettecbell.com for special deals, free fiction, and a list of series and reading orders. With over 100 complete series and counting, you'll never have to wait for your favorite read again.